THE HEROIN CHRONICLES

THE
HEROIN
CHRONICLES

WITHDRAWN

EDITED BY **JERRY STAHL**

Published by Akashic Books
©2013 Akashic Books

ISBN-13: 978-1-61775-106-6
Library of Congress Control Number: 2012939269

The story "Godhead" by Eric Bogosian was published in an earlier form in *The Essential Bogosian* (Theatre Communications Group, 1994).

Akashic Books
PO Box 1456
New York, NY 10009
info@akashicbooks.com
www.akashicbooks.com

TABLE OF CONTENTS

introduction
modes of desperation
by jerry stahl

> *It has not been in the pursuit of pleasure that I have periled life*
> *and reputation and reason. It has been the desperate attempt to*
> *escape from torturing memories, from a sense of insupportable*
> *loneliness and a dread of some strange impending doom.*
> —Edgar Allan Poe

S omewhere, a long time ago, I wrote: *All my heroes were junkies.* (Hey, you pick your cliché and you run with it. That's half of life.) So let's march 'em out. The Junkie All-Stars: Miles Davis, Lenny Bruce, Keith Richards, Billie Holliday, William S. Burroughs, even Dylan, there for a while. (Not to mention Cliff Edwards, otherwise known as Ukulele Ike, the voice of Jiminy Cricket and a lifelong addict. Junkies have all the best stories. But we'll get to that.)

Of course, Rush Limbaugh seems to have also colonized his hefty keister onto the Heavyweight Fiend list, but that's these days. (And we're not going to hoist up Herman Goering, another fat-ass fascist, and drag him around the track.) Oxycontin, known to newshounds, aficionados, and Justified fans as Hillbilly Heroin, is so much easier to acquire and imbibe than the old-fashioned nonprescription variety.

But don't get me wrong, I'm not judging Rush. A man's got to do what a man's got to do. And there is no finer cure to self-hate than determined, euphoria-inducing opiate use.

Culturally speaking—shout out to Rush again!—opiate consumption now packs all the glamour of the buttock boil that kept the right-wing rant-meister out of Vietnam. For which, perhaps, Drug Czar R. Gil Kerlikowske could issue a gold medal for yeoman service in the name of addiction prevention. And I say this with respect. Growing up, if some right-wing pork roast had morphed into our national dope fiend, I would have found another line of work and become an alcoholic. Everybody knows the difference between them: An alcoholic will steal your wallet in a blackout and apologize when he finds out. A junkie will steal it and help you look for it. Call it a matter of style, or a mode of desperation. Nothing wrong with *Lost Weekend* or *Arthur* or *Days of Wine and Roses*, but give me *Panic in Needle Park*, *Man with the Golden Arm*, and *Requiem for a Dream* any day.

Ply Mother Theresa with appletinis for three days straight and she'll crawl out the other end with dry mouth and a hangover. Shoot her up for three days and by Day Four the saint of Calcutta will be strung out like a lab monkey, ready to blow the mailman for dime-bag money. Being a junkie is not a lifestyle choice—it's an imperative of molecular chemistry.

Still, Keith, Miles, and Lenny made it look pretty cool. (Even if, one learns the hard way, Lou Reed and Bird aren't on hand to tamp your forehead with a wet towel when you're kicking. By which point it's pretty clear that heroin, at the proverbial end of the day, is about as glam as puking on your oatmeal.)

It may have been some twenty years since I've stuck a needle in my neck, but it's not like everything above it has healed up nicely. Shooting dope isn't what made me a crazy, pissed-off, outsider sleazeball and one-man crippling fear machine. Heroin just gave me an excuse. But that's me. If the short stories you are about to read in this collection are about nothing else, they're about actions—occasionally hell-driven, occasionally hilarious, uniformly desperation-and-delusion-fueled actions—the kind made by those in the grip of constant gnawing need. The entire anthology, on some level, can be viewed as an eclectic and festive encyclopedia of bad behavior.

But it's the need that makes the junkie a junkie. Even when it's not mentioned in any given story, it's there, like the weather, and it's always about to storm. Once the craving goes, the habit dissipates, but the dynamic—the Algebra of Need, as William S. Burroughs put it—remains in place. Junkies are like veterans, or bikers, or cancer survivors, or ex-cons. (Speaking just as a member of Team Dope Fiend, I don't trust anybody who hasn't been to hell. I may like you, I may even respect you, but, when the balls hit the griddle, I'd prefer somebody get my back who's had experience in my little neck of it. See, I know a guy, did a dime in Quentin. Been out twenty-three years. But even now—even now—according to his wife, he still wears prison sandals in the shower. Can't get wet barefoot. Once they've walked the yard, some men look over their shoulders their whole lives. Dope fiends, metaphorically or physically, live with their own brand of residual psychic baggage.)

When you're a junkie, you need junk to live. Everything's all on the line, all the time. Here's the thing: people know they're going to die—but junkies know what it feels like. They've kicked. Which hurts worse than death. But they know they're going to run out. It's a mind-set. No matter how big the pile on the table—junkies already see it gone. Junkies live under the Syringe of Damocles. Junkies exist as the anti-Nietzsches. Whatever doesn't kill you makes you need more dope.

Which doesn't make fiends unique—it makes them human. Just more so. Junkies feel too much. And need a lot to make them not feel.

Every writer you're about to read has been to places the "normal" human may not have been. And lived to talk about it. They haven't died for your sins. But they've felt like shit, in a variety of fascinating ways. And by the time you finish this fiction anthology, you will understand, from their pain, from their degradation, from their death-adjacent joy and skin-clawing, delirious three-a.m.-in-the-middle-of-the-day lows, the wisdom that comes from the nonstop drama and scarring comedy of living every second of your life in a race against the ticking clock of your own cells, a clock whose alarm is the sweaty, skin-scorching revelation that if you don't get what you need in three minutes your skin is going to burn and your bowels loosen, and whatever claim you had on dignity, self-respect, or power is going to drip down your leg and into your sock like the shaming wet shit of green-as-boiled-frog cold-turkey diarrhea.

Unlike serial killers or traditional torturers, junkies spend most of their time savaging themselves. That everyone they know and love in the world is often destroyed in the process is just a side issue. C.A.D. Collateral Addict Damage. *And yet.*

From this festive and inelegant hell, these junkie writers—some ex, some not-so-ex, but a good editor never tells—have returned with a kind of sclerosed wisdom. Their burning lives may lie scattered behind them like the remains of a plane crash in an open field, but the flames will, I guarantee, illuminate the lives of any and all who read it, whether addicted to dope, Jim Beam, gun shows, bus station sex, Mars bars, Texas Hold'em, telenovellas, fame or—thank you, Jesus, Lord of Weird Redemption—great fucking writing.

Jerry Stahl
Los Angeles, CA
September 2012

PART I
REALITY BLURS

TONY O'NEILL is the author of the novels *Sick City*, *Down and Out on Murder Mile*, and *Digging the Vein*, as well as several books of poetry and nonfiction. He does not blog or have a Facebook page. He misses the days when drug dealers had pagers. For more information, visit www.tonyoneill.net.

fragments of joe
by tony o'neill

My name is Joe, and I am an addict."

"Hi, Joe."

They were in a small church basement in East Holly-wood. The Wednesday-morning "Happy Hour" AA meeting was in full swing. Joe sat among a small group of ex-junkies, drunks, speed freaks, and crackheads, yet still looked like the sickest person in the room. A defeated-looking junkie in his late forties, Joe's face was patterned with deep creases and fresh sores. His eyes trembled in their sockets like two furtive crackheads hiding in a by-the-hour motel room.

At the back of the room was a woman called Tania, anxiously chewing a hangnail, watching the man who addressed the group. This was the second time she had noticed Joe at one of her regular meetings. Last week he was standing by the coffee urn at the Narcotics Anonymous near Hollywood and Highland, stuffing his pockets with stale cookies. And here he was today, addressing the group in a barely audible monotone, looking even worse than he had then.

Tania glanced around the room. She guessed she was the only person under thirty here, although sometimes with dope fiends you couldn't tell. This meeting attracted the old-timers, old fucks with years of sobriety under their belts who circled the newcomers like sharks around chum. She wasn't really sure why she had come here. She had already decided that this meeting would be her last. One last hour of her life just to be sure that this sobriety thing wasn't for her, and then she could return to the dealers at Bonnie Brae and 6th with a clean conscience and forty bucks in her pocket.

"Ahem," Joe said, "I don't feel good today. I relapsed again . . . a little while ago, you know? And it really took it out of me. I mean physically, it just took it out of me. Thing is, I'm finding it hard to even get the . . . *focus*, you know, the focus to begin the whole process again . . . to begin working on my recovery. I . . . I'm a heroin addict, as I'm sure some of you know." He gave a forced, self-effacing smile that didn't suit his face. "I had six months clean under my belt, but . . . right now I know I'm gonna struggle to even make it to the end of the day without using. I wasn't even planning on going to this meeting. I came here in a kind of *trance*, really. I dunno what else to do."

Tania wiped her nose with the back of her hand. Fuck, shit, piss. The meeting was a mistake. It's not as if her disillusionment with sobriety was a recent development. She'd been clean—and miserable as hell about it—for a good seven months now. The miracle they promised her never arrived. After the painful detox, expensive inpatient treatment, and her stint in that crummy sober living house, nothing was *better*. Everything was still shit. Every time she dragged her reluctant ass to a meeting, the stories of drug-induced degradation she heard just served to remind her of what she had given up. When someone like Joe came in, fresh from a relapse, she didn't feel *bad* for them. She secretly wished she had been getting high *with* them. Their sorry-ass apologies to the group just made the urge stronger.

Sober living had been a joke. Twenty-nine years old and forced to share a room with some dumb teenage methhead moron from Orange County, with perky tits and bad teeth. The bitch talked so much that Tania could only wonder what the hell she must have been like when she was doing crank. No, she'd decided as she'd hurriedly packed her bags last Sunday, I'm too old for this shit. Too smart. Something will come along.

". . . But I'm thankful to be here," Joe was saying. "And I'm going to keep trying . . . Thanks."

"Thanks, Joe."

Later they all stood, held hands, and said the serenity prayer. Years after her first meeting, Tania still felt the same indignation about the religious trappings of the program that she'd felt then. She didn't believe in God any more than she believed in redemption. They were stupid concepts, the kind of ideas that don't stand up to rational scrutiny. Plenty of people had told her to *fake it till you make it*. It was another of those irritating mantras that AA's true believers traded like baseball cards. But faking was never Tania's style.

Afterward, everybody broke into little groups to drink coffee, talk, and bullshit. Everyone except Joe. He headed straight for the door before anyone could try to intercept him. He was halfway down the block before Tania managed to catch up with him.

"Joe? Hey, *Joe!*"

He had the furtive gait of a shoplifter trying to walk away from the store as quickly—but nonchalantly—as possible. She thought for a moment that he was going to ignore her and simply keep walking. She called his name even louder this time. He paused.

"It's just like the song," she said, catching up to him.

Joe looked confused. "Song?"

"Hey Joe." Tania extended her hand. "I'm Tania."

"Oh, right. *That* song." After an awkward pause he finally took her hand and gave it a limp shake. "I'm . . ."

"You're Joe. I know." Tania removed her sunglasses. "D'you wanna go somewhere? I mean, with me?"

"Ah. Erm . . . well, I don't have time for coffee right now.

Thing is, I'm on my way to see someone, you know?"

Coffee. Another in a long fucking line of AA clichés. When someone seems like they're in trouble, on the verge of a relapse or a crisis of faith, someone else always drags them out for coffee and a pep talk. Tania had been through that routine more times than she could count.

"I don't *want* a coffee. Just wanna kill some time. Who you meeting?"

Despite her taste for narcotics and the lifestyle it had often forced her into, Tania still had a face. Six months away from the needle had given her a veneer of health. There was color in her cheeks, her breasts were filling out again as she put on a little sobriety weight. She wore a long-sleeved T-shirt despite the heat, with a picture of Marc Bolan emblazoned across it. Her hair was dyed black, with some blond poking through at the roots. Joe had not talked to a woman in what seemed like a lifetime. He felt like a tongue-tied teenage boy.

"I'm just meeting . . . he's just a friend of mine. No one special."

"Can he get something for me?"

"What do you mean?"

"You know."

"Yeah, maybe. Well . . . yeah."

"Then I wanna see your friend too. You wanna kill some time together, or what?"

"Uh-hum."

"Is that all right?"

"Look, Tania, I'm broke. I mean, I've only got enough bread to get straight with, you know."

"I'm not asking for a freebie. Just some company, that's all. Is that okay?"

Joe shrugged. "Yeah, I guess."

* * *

They drove downtown together in Joe's battered Honda. His connection operated out of a loft space near Pershing Square. They found an empty meter, and he brought her to a steel door sandwiched between a grimy-looking fried chicken joint and a store that sold Santería artifacts. Joe rang the buzzer and a voice crackled, *"Yeah?"*

"It's Joe, lemme in."

"Who'ssat with jou?"

"Friend of mine. She's cool."

The door buzzed open.

The damp concrete stairwell reeked of piss and bleach. When they almost reached the top they saw people lined up in front of them. They took their place behind two young punk girls in leather jackets and Dr. Martens, sniffling dejectedly. After a minute or two a sallow man wearing a Nike T-shirt and baseball cap clumped up the stairs and joined the line. They stood there, silently waiting for the line to move, with the cool detached manner of people waiting for a bathroom stall to open up. The guy behind them, who had a thick Russian accent, gave Joe a nudge and tried to make conversation.

"Fuck, man. I'm sick, yeah?"

Joe ignored him. Tania glanced over her shoulder and made eye contact. The guy pressed on.

"I get twenty-dollar balloon this morning. Won't even get me straight. I think his stuff getting worse, no?" The Russian wiped his runny nose with the back of his hand.

"Then why d'you come back here?" Tania asked.

"He . . . this man . . . is the only dealer I have!"

Tania glanced at Joe, who rolled his eyes and rested his head against the cool plaster.

They'd pooled their money. Eighty bucks. Two balloons of

dope, and the rest for rock. Enough to take the edge off the day. The door at the top of the stairs opened and a small, skinny Latino kid—no more than twelve or thirteen years old—emerged with a nervous-looking man in a business suit, who hurried down the stairs. The kid peered down the line, then took the punk girls' money. They followed him up the stairs and through the door. Joe and Tania took a few steps forward; she felt her guts churning in anticipation. It was really going to happen. Standing in the pissy stairwell, Joe seemed more solid, healthier, somehow more *real* than before. Now that he was in his natural element, it seemed to Tania that he had taken on an extra dimension. That craggy face could almost be taken for handsome, in a damaged kind of way. The minutes dragged by. The door opened, and the punks scurried down the stairs, chipmunk-faced, the drugs stashed in their cheeks. The kid now approached Joe, who handed him the bills and they followed him up.

"Whatchoo need?"

"Cuarenta negro, cuarenta blanco."

"Sí."

"It's good stuff?"

"What *good*? Is always good, jou know that."

"The same stuff as yesterday?"

"Yeah, man." They were at the door now. "Why jou askit this?"

Joe nodded faintly in the Russian's direction. "Guy down there said the chiva was malo. Said he didn't even get high from the stuff you sold him this morning."

The kid looked visibly agitated, and muttered under his breath in Spanish. "He crazy. Mess up in the head. Always ask for credit. Get mad when we say no, jou know? Makit *trouble*."

"So it's the same as last time?"

"Sí. Is the same."

"A'right. Cool."

The kid opened the door. The room beyond was a huge, desolate loft space. The only furnishings were a TV with an Xbox attached, a leather couch, and a coffee table. The windows were covered with black sheets. A bald man-mountain wearing a Lakers top sat with his back to them, engrossed in a game of *Grand Theft Auto*, a gun casually poking out of the waistband of his shorts. Two other guys, dressed in chinos and button-down check shirts, on the couch. One bald with a wispy mustache. The other with long, straggly hair and a goatee. On the table was a shoebox full of money. Next to it two handguns, a weighing scale, and a copy of *Trump: How to Get Rich*. The guy with the goatee was expertly wrapping preweighed lumps of tar heroin in wax paper, stuffing them into tiny black balloons, and tying them off. The young kid handed the money to the mustache. He counted it and put it into the shoebox without a word. They talked among themselves in Spanish without looking at Joe and Tania as they handed the kid the drugs. The kid passed the stuff to Joe, and he popped it in his mouth.

The kid led them back to the door, pulled back the deadbolt, turned a handle, and wrenched it open. There was a sudden rush of activity. It took Tania a moment to realize what was happening. The Russian, snot still streaming down his nose, had barged in and grabbed the kid by the shirt, pressing a pistol against his head.

"Getouttathefuckingway!" he screamed.

Joe grabbed Tania and dragged her to the side. They huddled for safety against a wall while the Russian marched the kid back into the room and started barking orders.

"Everybody up! This is a fucking robbery! On your feet. You, fatso! Toss over the gun or I blow his head off. No bullshit!"

The big guy stopped playing the Xbox, and slowly reached around and pulled the gun out of his waistband. Without turning around he gently placed it on the ground, sliding it across the floor a little. Then he rotated on his ass to face the Russian. The other two were sitting there with looks of outraged disbelief on their faces.

"Kick the gun over, fatso! And you two—on your feet or I shoot him. Hands in the air, quick, quick!"

From her vantage, Tania could see the Russian clearly. His hand was trembling. He was dope sick and desperate. By contrast, the dealers were cool as hell. Even the kid with the gun pressed against his temple seemed nonplussed. They all moved with a kind of insect calm, slowly doing whatever the Russian instructed. Waiting for the right opportunity to pounce. Tania sensed that the Russian was too nervous, too desperate to pull this off. She closed her eyes.

"Okay, everyone against the wall."

They lined up silently. They stood there, palms up, watching the guy closely as if committing every aspect of his face to memory.

"Jou really focked up," the goatee muttered.

"Shut up! Fucking beaner!"

"Jou robbing 18th Street, homie." The goatee shook his head sadly. "They gonna cut off jou balls."

"One more fucking word outta you and I'll kill him, and then I'll kill you. Yeah?"

The goatee shrugged.

The Russian glanced toward Joe and Tania, still huddling together next to the door. "You on the floor. You, bitch!"

Tania looked up.

"Listen. You need to get up slowly, no sudden movements. I want you to go over to the table and pick up the dope. Put it all in the shoebox with the money. Close it up and bring it over to me. Don't fuck around."

'Joe squeezed her hand and whispered, "It's okay. Just be cool."

Tania did as she was told. She brought the box over, stopping a good three feet away from the Russian. She realized she needed to piss badly and a mad urge to laugh came over her. She watched the Russian's hand trembling wildly, the muzzle of the gun twitching against the young kid's temple.

"Now what?" she whispered.

"Put the box down and slide it over."

She did this. The box lay just in front of the Russian and the kid he was holding hostage.

"Now go. Back over there."

Tania scurried to Joe, crouched down with him again. As they huddled Joe could feel her trembling. He whispered, "It's gonna be okay." Somehow she believed him.

The Russian sniffed, more and more snot dripping down his face. "Okay, that's good. This is what's going to happen. Me and my friend here are going to go down the stairs. If anyone even peeks their head out of the door before I'm on the street, I shoot him. I'm not bullshiting, in Russia I've kill *many* men in cold blood. I'm no fucking joke. Asshole," he said, poking the gun harder against the kid's temple. "We bend down together. On three. You pick up the box, and we get out of here. Yes?"

The kid remained silent. His young face may as well have been carved in stone.

"Okay. This is one . . . two . . . and . . . and . . ."

A look of confusion came over the Russian's face. His nose and mouth twitched wildly, as if he were having some kind of facial spasm. "Ah," he bleated. He sniffed as more goop dripped from his nose. "Ah!" he said again. He wrinkled his nose wildly. "*Ahhh* . . ."

The Russian sneezed. The sound of it—and the almost instantaneous bang as the gun went off—echoed around the loft. The kid flew sideways, the contents of his skull exploded from the side of his face. When Tania opened her eyes again, the Russian was just standing there, his face slick with blood, holding the gun with a look of terrified confusion. He stared at the murder weapon as if seeing it in his hand for the first time. He peered down at the kid. He was laying with half his face blown off, in a rapidly expanding pool of blood.

"Shit!" the Russian screamed at his hand, as if it had betrayed him. "SHIT!" He looked up. The three dealers were already advancing on him. He turned the trembling gun on them. Screamed, "Back off!" They stopped advancing.

"Jou a fockin' dead man," the biggest of them said. "Jou shot my focking cousin. You fockin' dead man."

The Russian kept the gun on them, glancing down to the bloody shoebox, then over to the door, as if weighing his options. Tania thought he might be crazy enough to try and grab the box and outrun the dealers. Suddenly the Russian's hand stopped shaking and a strange calm seemed to settle over him.

"No," he said, firmly. "*You're* a fucking dead man."

He opened fire, setting off a series of deafening cracks as bullets flew around the room. One caught the big man in the chest, another hit the mustache in the groin, a third blasted the goatee in the stomach. All three hit the ground. The two who were still alive were screaming and cursing in Spanish. The Russian stood over them and used his last two bullets to put them out of their misery. He tucked the gun in his waistband and went over to the table. He grabbed the dealers' guns and then retrieved the bloodstained shoebox. Almost as an afterthought he paused on his way out and told Joe and Tania to get on their feet. They did not get up. The Russian looked at them with a curious expression on his face.

"We didn't see nothing, man," Joe said. "Look, we just wanna get the fuck outta here and go get high, that's all. We ain't going to the fucking cops or telling anyone we were here. Okay?"

The Russian nodded slowly. Then he pulled one of the dealers' guns and fired four times. The first two bullets hit Joe in the stomach. The third hit Tania in the chest. The fourth went wild, ricocheting around the room. He fired again, but there was the click of an empty chamber. Joe and Tania lay over each other, a pile of tangled limbs and hot, fresh blood. With that, the Russian fled down the stairs.

"I'm sorry," Tania said.

"What're you sorry about?"

"Peeing. I peed in my fuckin' pants, can't you smell it? It's probably on your upholstery. I'm so . . . *ugh*."

"Don't sweat it."

They were in Joe's car, heading back to Hollywood. Smoking cigarettes with still-trembling fingers. It wasn't shock or fear that made their hands shake. Instead it was something that felt like the aftermath of a particularly strong orgasm.

"What the fuck do you think just happened?"

Joe looked over to Tania. She stared off into space, but didn't answer. She just carried on smoking, and looking down impassively at the gaping, bloody hole in her shirt. She shook her head slowly.

"I mean," Joe said in a voice that was a mixture of horror and wonder, "I mean just *look* at me!"

She looked over and her eyes widened, as if she were seeing the devastation for the first time. With one hand still on the wheel, Joe lifted his bloody shirt. His stomach was ripped open, his jeans soaked with deep black blood. Something that looked like a purple, flayed snake lolled obscenely out of the moist hole. It lay glistening on his lap. She shook her head dreamily.

"Tania . . . did we *die*?"

Tania half closed her eyes and let her head rest lazily against the passenger window, as they turned down Wilcox Avenue.

"I don't know. All I know is that it felt . . ." She drifted off, a wan smile playing on her lips.

"Amazing?" Joe whispered.

"Yeah. It felt fucking *amazing*."

As soon as they made it back to her room at the Gilbert Hotel, they got high. It was a run-down box with threadbare brown carpeting and a broken television bolted to the wall. When they stumbled in past the front desk, Joe holding his guts in with his forearm, the old Bangladeshi man behind the Plexiglas window with the *NO GUESTS NO EXCEPTIONS* sign pasted to it didn't look up from his newspaper.

Tania locked the door behind them while Joe busily cooked up a bag of dope in a bottle cap. He took off his shirt and wrapped it around his abdomen as a temporary fix.

"Got any vitamin C?"

"Yeah, think so."

"Lemme see a pill."

She threw over a bright orange pill from the bottle in the bathroom. Joe examined it for a moment, and nodded. He clumsily crushed half the pill into powder against the bedside cabinet, then sprinkled it into the heroin. He dropped a healthy chunk of crack into the dark brown goop and heated it again. Tania watched him curiously.

"You need an acid to break down the rock. Otherwise you can shoot it. You got a spike?"

Tania shook her head.

"I got a fresh one. You can go first if you want. You ain't got hep or nuthin', do you?"

"No." She glanced down at her T-shirt, which was plastered to her body with drying blood. "But I guess it wouldn't matter at this point, would it?"

"Guess not."

She watched him rip open the syringe and draw some of the caramel-colored mixture into it through a cigarette filter.

"Jesus, Joe. Be careful . . . I haven't had a fix in over a year . . ."

"You worried you're gonna OD or something? Like you said, probably wouldn't matter at this point, Tania."

Joe offered to hit Tania. After she got her fix, she watched him shoot up with all the practiced efficiency of an old-timer. While it felt pretty good, Tania couldn't help but think that the speedball was somehow disappointing. Shooting dope seemed pretty anticlimactic after experiencing death in all of its terrible, wonderful glory. It reminded Tania of when she had smoked crack for the first time. How alien the idea that she could ever just *snort* coke again suddenly seemed. It was instantly rendered pointless, a monstrous waste of drugs.

As Joe and Tania lay in the aftermath of their speedballs in that squalid Hollywood hotel room, they each realized intuitively that something about them had been changed forever. There was no going back to the old ways now.

Four days later, Joe lay on the floor of his apartment on Normandie and Franklin. He was puking yellow goo into a bowl that was already full to the brim with foul-smelling bile. He was shaking violently. His guts were hastily held together with layer upon layer of CVS bandages and duct tape, and each time he retched he became paranoid that they would rip apart and his insides would come spilling out again. The phone rang. He looked at the digital clock glowing on the cable box. It was two thirty a.m. He crawled over and retrieved the handset.

"Um," he mumbled. "Eh. Hello?"

"Joe? Oh God, Joe, is that you?"

"Yeah . . . I'm here, Tania."

"Joe!" She sounded like she was crying. "I'm sick! I'm fucking sick. I don't understand it. It started last night. It's getting worse . . . I bought a bottle of fucking methadone . . . drank the lot . . . nothing *helps* . . ."

He listened as she vomited violently. He tried his best to sound comforting, shushing her gently until her convulsions seemed to recede.

"I know . . . I know . . . I shot some dope two hours ago, didn't do a thing. I can't get this sickness to go . . . I've never been this sick . . . Never . . ."

They listened to each other groan and sigh over the phone for a while. Their pain seemed to eventually give away to an exhausted surrender to the futility and horror of it all.

"Joe. I'm coming over. I need to get well."

"Okay." He gave her directions, in between retches. "Hurry, okay?"

"Okay."

Forty-five minutes later she stumbled out of a cab and staggered toward the apartment building. Finding Joe's door, she pounded frantically until he yanked it open. He was stooped over, like a little old man. The apartment was dark, and smelled of sickness and rotting meat. She couldn't tell if the smell was from Joe's apartment, or if it was rising from her own fetid wound. They embraced painfully.

"How're we gonna do this?" she gasped in his sweat-drenched mop of hair.

"The bathroom . . ."

Tania let her heavy coat fall to the floor, exposing a David Bowie shirt soaked crimson. She staggered after Joe. The fluorescent lights momentarily burned her eyes. He was standing there, pointing to the bathtub. It was full of water. An extension chord snaked in from the living room. An ancient twelve-inch black-and-white TV sat on the toilet's lid.

"This'll be the easiest way. The quickest. And it won't make a mess like the fucking bullets did."

"Yeah. I guess that's smart."

As if to emphasize the point Tania pulled off her T-shirt. Right between her tits, in the space where the bullet had gone in, was a wad of surgical cotton the size of a fist. It was stuffed into the wound and stained a gruesome shade of brown. It was clumsily held in place with peeling duct tape.

"I'm still scared," she said.

"I know."

"I mean, what if we don't come back this time? Or what if we do, but it doesn't *fix* us?"

Joe shrugged. "Could it be any worse than feeling like this?"

"No. I guess not."

Joe and Tania undressed silently. There was no embarrassment. There is nothing two people can share that is more intimate than death. They folded their clothes into neat piles and placed them by the sink, grimly focused on the task at hand. Tania went in first. Joe held her hand as she climbed into the lukewarm water. She sat at one end of the tub with her knees pressed tightly together. The water began to turn pink. Joe gingerly eased himself into the tub after her.

His bandages soaked through quickly. The bathwater steadily deepened from pink into a murky scarlet.

"Does it hurt?" Tania had a look of almost motherly concern on her face.

"Not the wound. Everything else hurts, but not the fucking wound."

"Fucking same thing here."

Joe reached over and flicked the TV on. A repeat of *Entertain-*

ment Tonight was playing. Mark Steines was talking about Lindsay Lohan.

"Turn it down, Joe. If this doesn't work I don't want this shit to be the last thing I hear."

Joe muted the channel.

"Here we go."

Joe picked up the TV and

Dropped

It

In

The

Tub

There was a flash of intense white, a strobelike flicker, and then nothing. Lights instantly went out all over the apartment building.

And then it was over.

Joe came out of it first. The house was shrouded in darkness. The air smelled funny. In the dark, he could see the television floating in the water between them. The water was brown and fetid. They had shat themselves at the moment of death. It didn't matter. Tania started to stir, lifting her chin from her chest. Joe smiled a slow, satisfied smile.

"How do you feel?"

Tania let out a long, ecstatic sigh. "Fucking *fantastic*. You got a cigarette?"

There was a faint smell of cooking meat in the air. Joe placed a hand on his hair and it felt brittle, singed. But the unbelievable relief that he felt was better than anything he had ever experienced in his entire life. As they both sat there in a tub full of electrified water and shit, coasting on their high, they started to slowly nod off into a gentle dream state.

* * *

"My name is Joe, and I'm an addict."

"*Hi, Joe.*"

"I'm finding it impossible to quit. I've had three relapses in as many weeks. I know they say to *keep coming back* but : . . I'm sick right now. It's been two days since my last relapse. I'm here because it's all I can think to do . . ."

As Joe talked, Tania sat next to him, watching. She didn't tell him, but this morning as he lay passed out on Valium, she'd silently crept into the bathroom and looked at herself in the mirror. Withdrawal sweat was soaking every inch of her stick-thin body. Her tits looked a cup-size smaller. She reminded herself of those awful pictures of Nazi concentration camp survivors. The hole in her chest wasn't healing. In fact, it was starting to smell worse and no matter what she stuffed in there—cotton, old newspapers—the stench still leaked out from under her clothes. She had even tried an air freshener inside the rotting cavern, but that uneasy mixture of decay and potpourri was somehow worse.

What use was this if the body couldn't heal itself afterward? She had been shitting blood for four days since the last reckless, desperate fix. She had gulped down a bottle of drain cleaner in a moment of feverish madness. This morning, with the sickness back worse than ever, she *had* to do something about it. Joe was insisting that they detox and she'd initially agreed, and now he was watching her for signs of weakness. It was like being back in that fucking sober living house. Back to the cycle of meetings, prayers, and self-denial. She couldn't stand it. Joe could stick out his attempt at doing it cold turkey if that's what he really wanted. After all, she rationalized, how could she help him with his own detox if she was incapacitated by sickness? If she could just stay well enough to help him, then maybe he stood a better chance of actually making it. *Then* she would detox. Her mind made up, this morning she had a fix without telling Joe. She carefully slid the kitchen knife up into the hole in her chest, and stabbed around in there until she hit paydirt. When she came to on the bathroom floor, she finally felt human again.

Joe's words of pain and sickness washed over her as she sat in the AA meeting later that day. Even the old-timers, the lifelong drinkers with red noses and rotted teeth and dead livers, looked at this bedraggled pair with a mixture of pity and concealed disgust.

"... And that's it. I'm going to keep going. I'm going to try and break my addiction this time. Thanks for listening."

"*Thanks, Joe.*"

"*Keep coming back!*"

"*One day at a time!*"

Afterward they walked back toward the Hollywood and Western Metro. The car had been towed, after being illegally parked for two days.

"I feel like shit," Joe said. "I want to die."

Tania summoned up her best "sick" face. "Yeah. Me too."

"You lying fucking *bitch*. You're high as a fucking kite. Don't give me that shit."

"I'm not high! Honestly, Joe!"

She reached out to him, but he shrugged her away. He moved ahead of her, down into the station. She caught up to him as he hissed, "Don't try and bullshit me, all right? I can see it all over your damn face. You were nodding out in that fucking meeting."

Down on the platform, Tania stood next to Joe feeling like a chastised kid. She felt guilty, ashamed of her lies. On the display it said the next train to Pershing Square would arrive in one minute. She looked over at Joe. He was ashen. A droplet of sweat was forming on his nose. Even though the platform was pretty crowded, the people gave the two of them the wide berth usually reserved for the dangerously insane, or the stinking homeless. Black wind gusted through the tunnel as a train approached.

"Tania?" Joe said in a quiet voice.

"Yeah?"

"I'm sorry."

And then Joe was gone. He stepped forward, straight off the platform. For a moment it looked like he was suspended in the air. He looks like Wile E. Coyote, Tania thought for a shell-shocked moment, before Joe tumbled forward, then vanished completely as the train whooshed past her.

Thhhhhuuuuuddddddddd!

The impact carried Joe away. The scream of brakes and the yells of shocked commuters echoed around the station as Joe flew off in a hail of blood. Tania felt it hit her in the face, like some obscene custard-pie gag. Joe's insides splashed across the face of a screaming woman next to her with the impact of an open-handed slap. The woman fell to the floor screaming, covered in gore.

People were running around in confusion. The train came to a stop halfway into the tunnel, with Joe's mangled corpse caught in the wheels, ripped into meaty fragments across the track, shredded and starting to cook in the hot crevices of the brake levers. In the mayhem, nobody noticed a silent, decaying woman silently make her way off of the platform.

She considered following Joe into the path of an oncoming train in the weeks that followed. As the sickness worsened, Tania found that the quickest, easiest way to do it was asphyxiation. The biggest problem was that when she held the plastic bag tight over her head, and the heat started to build as she instinctively gasped for breath, the urge to tear the bag off was almost unbearable. It took several attempts before she was able to see it through for the first time. After that, Tania was a pro. Once you rode out those two or three minutes of panic, death came on slow and easy, like sliding into a warm bath. Instead of rotting wounds or a bleeding anus, she was left with a red face—the result of the blood vessels constantly erupting under her skin. But she looked no worse, she supposed, than many of the alcoholics she had met at the meetings.

But still, she did consider doing what Joe did. Maybe it would be easier to just cease to *be*, once and for all. The rush was becoming less and less, and the withdrawal symptoms seemed to intensify with each passing week. The past few months she had become a ghost, a shell, something that existed only in the shadows.

A month or so later, something happened that made her change her mind about following Joe. She was visiting the quiet section of Griffith Park where she'd spread Joe's ashes. She was just sitting there, watching the sky as the golden hour began to fade. The place was silent, peaceful. The noise and heat of the city may as well have been a million miles away. It was in this fleeting moment that she thought she heard it, an almost subliminal noise carried softly to her in the breeze.

Tania . . .
Taaania . . .
Pleasssee . . .
Pleasse . . .
Just one more fix . . .
And then I'll quit . . .
For goood . . .

The tears came then, as she finally understood the true extent of Joe's hell. She imagined him reduced by a crematorium's violent heat to a billion little ashes, countless tiny fragments of carbon, dumped out of an urn and left to flit around in the careless breeze.

She imagined Joe clinging to the underside of plants and trees, lost in discarded beer cans, and stuck in piles of fresh dog shit. And all of those infinitesimal specks of what he once was still burning with that terrible sickness, that unimaginable yearning, a billion fragments of Joe still futilely screaming out for the relief of a fix he could never have again.

Tania stood stiffly, and addressed the breeze: "Goodbye, Joe. I'm sorry. I can't help you anymore. I've got my own habit to feed."

And then she was gone. As the sun sank behind the hills, the park fell into miserable, pensive silence once more.

Jazzmine Beaulieu

SOPHIA LANGDON grew up in Tampa, Florida, and moved to New York City in 2003. She is a writer of short fiction and a poet. She is currently working on a short story collection titled *What's Normal About Love?* and two books of poetry, *Love Letters to My Master* and *Is This How the World Turns Out*. She can be seen performing selections of her poetry at various venues throughout New York City.

hot for the shot
by sophia langdon

Eliza stepped with light protracted steps to the bathroom two feet away from their bed, and headed toward the stash she had been hiding: her old cottons. She looked back at him as she closed the door. He was asleep. She was thankful for that. She didn't want him to be awake, his eyes searching for her next move, looking for what he could get.

She did everything with awareness of every creak, every footfall. She didn't want to share. There wouldn't be enough. She reached into the medicine cabinet, took one tampon from the back row of many, pulled it from the cardboard applicator, and emptied the hardened pelts of cotton hidden behind it into her hand. The faucet clacked and chattered. She stood unmoving for a moment, listening. Then let the dribbling of water fill a white top from a water bottle. She added the cotton stones, watching them soften and bloom. It would be a shot of mostly cool water in her veins. She began the extraction, hoping for gold. Hoping whatever made it into the syringe would take the edge off, get her a little well—it wouldn't. She would once again be the victim of her exaggerated memory.

Eliza settled onto the rim of the tub, her legs straight, locked against the door. The syringe in her mouth held in place by lip and teeth, she wrapped her hand tight around her upper arm, pumping her fist, searching for a welcome spot in the crook of her arm. She stuck the needle in, a little blood came swirling out, the edge got fuzzy. But it didn't disappear. She got up from her perch and began to clean up: syringe flushed with water and back in the cup with their toothbrushes, he would know, but she would at least make an effort.

Eliza caught her reflection in the mirror and held her own gaze. Her eyes maintained a permanent shade of fading pink, sharp high cheekbones held up her taut, hollow, brown skin. Her face littered with black spots. Souvenirs from scratching and picking, God knows what else.

"I don't look so bad. Nothing makeup can't hide." The mistake of her words hit her before she had time to find solace in her own sophism. She pulled back her long, black, thick hair—still strong. She let it fall down her back. Something to flick and play with, she thought, something for the johns to hold onto. She smiled, and too many black spaces where once there were teeth smiled back. "Fuck, I'm too young." She gripped the side of the sink, then let go, walking carelessly out of the bathroom.

His eyes glazed with sleep, yet questioning, met her. His gaze traveled the distance between where he sat at the edge of the bed, to the dribble of blood rolling down her arm. "What about me? Where's my fucking breakfast? I'd like to wake up, roll over, and get high too."

"Fuck you, Eli."

Eliza walked to the faux kitchen—a counter, a sink, a hot plate—and began to wash dishes; an assortment of kept takeout food containers, a seemingly endless supply of spoons, and a pot. Their apartment was the first in a row of the shiniest-little-shit-holes along Fifth Avenue in Ybor City, Tampa Bay. Eli's vocation of dishwasher had kept them in deluxe digs for a while, before he managed to get fired from almost every restaurant on the ten-mile stretch of the Seventh Avenue strip. Now they worked together selling themselves, usually Eliza's self, whatever it took to maintain their habits and the lifestyle.

"Roll over and get high is all you ever do, you fuck," Eliza mumbled.

"What!"

"I didn't say anything."

Eli stumbled around, checking the empty dope bags and gum wrappers that littered the apartment floor, wanting a miracle of found glory.

Eliza finished up in the kitchen. She put on her self-styled lime-green and fluorescent-pink floral-print mini-muumuu, slipped on her white platform flip-flops, and headed for the door. "I'll be right back."

"Where are you going?"

"To Brett's."

Brett was their sixty-plus-year-old neighbor. He was rumored to be a plumber, but they had never seen him head out to a job in the two years they had known him or the three they had lived on shiny-shit-hole row. Five feet and scarcely an inch more, Brett was just tall enough to not be a midget. His face, and his disposition, gave you the sense that someone had started punching him when he was three, and just kept on hitting. Brett was always good for pills after a blowjob or a quick fuck. And this morning he was the only hope for her and bright-eyed Eli making it through the day's obligations. Obligations that wouldn't be met without chemical motivation, obligations necessary to get funding for things owed, and things hoped for, from Moses, their drug dealer—referred to as PRDD (Puerto Rican Drug Dealer) or the Biblical Bringer, depending on the day and their level of admiration for what he had to offer. Right now, all they had was her pussy, her mouth, and a pill-popping plumber to ensure they wouldn't be shivering on a street corner.

Eliza muttered as she walked to Brett's. "It will be quick. It always is." When she arrived she made small talk filled with innuendo: "Haven't had my morning pounding. Eli's wet as a noodle, scouring the place for something."

"Uhuh."

"God knows what he figures he'll find. All I can think about is how I woke up with a need to be filled that's still as empty as the bags he keeps checking through."

"Uhuh."

She stopped chattering long enough to grab them both beers from the fridge. She sat on Brett's lap, rubbing his cock through his pants, her mouth pressed to his ear. "You willing to help my greedy little cunt?"

"You're too much." A half-cocked grin on his face, Brett pulled her close and ran his tongue across her lips, parted them with it, and began to kiss her. He was gentle, in that way that lonely discarded men always are.

Eliza unzipped his pants. Brett sucked in, his breath caught up by his need to fuck, to believe that she wanted him. She spat on her hand, lifted her dress, and stuck her lubricated fingers into her pussy. His hands followed hers. Fingers shoving into her well-trained holes. She moaned, and told him how badly she needed him to fuck her. He stood up and she laid on the dingy, cracked linoleum floor. She could feel the dirt rubbing into her skin. Her body called him down, no more need for words as she watched him remove his pants. Brett was short and the engagement would be shorter, but he was hung; God's obscene joke to make a man equipped but inadequate. The initial entry pleased her, made her gasp even, but it was sure to leave her wanting more. Two minutes tops. He got up and went to the bathroom. He always had to take a shit after sex. She didn't try or care to analyze it. The closing of the door was like a starter's pistol. She moved quickly, making her way back to his room.

His shelves didn't contain knickknacks, or clothes, or books, just rows and rows of pill bottles with various names of patients and doctors. It was a fucking pharmacy, a pill junkie's dream, an endless row of tiny tubs in varying states. She filled the deep pockets of her muumuu with Oxycontin, Vicodin, Percocet, Adderall, random barbiturates, and uppers whose names she'd never remember. She left while Brett was still launching shit rockets into the toilet.

As she walked to the 7-Eleven a block away, Eliza wondered if Brett knew that she was ripping him off. Maybe he went to the bathroom so she wouldn't have to beg, knowing his own fiendish propensities wouldn't allow him to simply give her the pills. It was the sort of silly romantic notion she always tried to believe—soft, false truths.

The guy behind the counter was the little brother of a friend from high school. A remainder from when she was headed toward success, he still reacted to her as if she were the key to hallway royalty. She wondered, did he want to fuck her or did he just feel a need to be polite, respecting what she used to be? He let her use the bathroom, he pretended not to notice when she was stealing, he generally gave her the run of the place.

"Tommy. How's your sister doing?" She never really stopped her forward motion to the bathroom.

Eliza filled her cupped hands with water and slurped it into her mouth. She pushed Vicodin and Oxycontin in between her clenched lips. She sat on the toilet and removed the cache of drugs from her pockets, picked out Oxys, Vicodins, Percocets, wrapped them up and tucked her package between the lips of her snatch. She patted the bulge between her legs. "Rainy-day stash." She flushed the toilet, a silly pretense, a game of making believe the store clerk didn't know.

She walked back to the apartment, the edge gone, her world a blurry sort of perfection. Occasionally patting her twat as she went, making sure her stash was still in place.

"Hey, baby, I got some pills: Vikes, Percocet, various randoms."

"You didn't get no Oxy?"

"No, the bottle was empty."

"Maybe he hid them when he heard your ass at the door. Did you come this time before your lover hopped off?"

"Fuck you."

Eliza emptied the contents of her pockets onto the coffee table, and grabbed her outfit for the day: denim miniskirt, white vintage Victorian top with cutoff sleeves and intricate folds running from the shoulders down the breast. She headed for the bathroom and counted five before doing anything. Eli busted in. She looked up from the water running into the showerless tub.

"What?"

He rolled his eyes. "Hand me my kit."

Eliza pulled the suburban-douche-bag leather kit, a junkie status symbol, out of the medicine cabinet and handed it to him. She closed the door, retrieved the package from her panties. She separated out the Vikes, Percocet, Adderall, set them on the flat edge of the sink, splashed water in the tub to feign activity, sat for a moment waiting for him to enter again. Feeling safe now, she began refilling her hollowed-out tampon with the booty of Oxycontin, and wedged it into its space at the back of the box. The other pills went into her skirt pocket. When she exited the bathroom, her eyes were surprised by the two lonely Vicodin waiting for her on the coffee table. She looked from the pills to Eli.

"Baby, you know you don't need as much as me to get high. Don't worry, I didn't do them all, I put some away for us."

"Uhuh." This motherfucker, she thought, he'll never be high enough, shoot your life into his arm and he'll still be searching for the next. She stepped in front of the floor-length mirror next to their bed. Eli went into the bathroom. She visualized him checking the medicine cabinet, hoping she'd covered her trail. Her eyes caught the clock: it had somehow become twelve thirty and they had to be in Lutz by two. They'd be late for the shoot.

She grabbed the phone. The lady who answered introduced herself as Ann-Marie. "Hi, this is Eliza, your two o'clock. We're running a little late."

"If you can't make it by three, forget shooting today."

"No worries, we'll definitely be there before three."

Eliza hung up the phone and watched the not so freshly washed Eli as he pulled on her old tattered Diesel jeans, the denim tight around his stick-thin legs, which seemed to take up most of his six-two frame, and a black cowboy shirt meant for a child, the sleeves too short. He was checking himself out, mussing his hair to a tumbled perfection, fashion choices being assessed from the tips of his pointy black shoes to the last well-managed strand of hair. He was handsome. Piercing blue eyes jumped out from the paleness of his skin at a stark juxtaposition to his jet-black hair, eyebrowless face, and perfect, full, pouty, fuck-and-suck lips. She didn't dare to say it, didn't want to give him the satisfaction of hearing it.

"Hurry up."

He grabbed her by the waist, stood her in front of him, pulling her hair back and kissing her neck. "Damn, we look good together baby." He lifted her short denim skirt, simultaneously pulling the fabric of her panties into the crack of her ass. He turned her around to look at the perfect roundness gripped in his hands. The curve of her back met the meaty suppleness of it. He lifted and held it, squeezing. She stood on the tips of her baby blue Chucks. He could feel his cock getting hard and he passed his fingers along the wetness of her cunt. She shivered just a little.

"Baby, you want me to fuck you?"

She pulled away. "We'll be late."

"Okay." He smacked her ass as she walked away from him.

Eliza grabbed her purse and the car keys off the nightstand. She stopped at the door, fanned a little air into her panties, and walked out. All the pills hit her as the sunshine seeped into her skin. She pulled her hair up into a loose chignon mimic of a bun with a black twisty-tie, before getting into the white mini–station wagon and turning the air-conditioning on full blast to fight the Florida heat. She watched the apartment door Eli had just rushed back through to get the directions their connection had given them. He waved the paper around as he came out.

Eli threw himself into the driver's seat.

"You okay to drive?" she asked.

She knew she wasn't. The pills were in control. She handed Eli the keys. They headed up Seventh toward Martin Luther King Boulevard, took that to the toll road, and got on. The car was gliding down the expressway when there was a loud boom. They looked around for a moment before realizing it was the sound of them hitting the railing along the side of the highway. Eliza snapped out of her stupor as the car screeched and scraped along the rail. Eli, his foot pushing the brake to floor, was trying to pull away and regain control. The car came to an abrupt stop. He looked over at her, his eyes stretched wide with fear and surprise.

"What the fuck! I thought you were okay to drive!"

"I am. I sorta fell asleep." He smirked, and they both started to laugh.

The little white, and now steel-gray, station wagon was banged up good. The driver's-side door wouldn't open. Eliza got out and took a look. Eli peered inquisitively at her through the windshield before sliding across the seat and getting out of the car, the air-conditioning blasting, the radio blaring, the engine still running. They stood stupefied glancing back and forth between the car and each other, shook their heads, and shrugged before walking around to get back in. Eli slid behind the wheel. Eliza got in after him, slammed the door, and looked at the time on the dashboard clock.

"Come on. Let's get out of here. It's already fucking three thirty. We can't miss this."

Eli smiled, revved the engine, and absentmindedly tweaked the key in the ignition making the car squeal. Knowing that neither of them would pass even the suggestion of a sobriety test, they took off, looking back to make sure no one had been called to check on their welfare. Forty minutes later they were pulling up at a ranch-style house with an immaculate yard, the peek of a screened-in pool enclosure beyond the rooftop.

"You sure this is it?" asked Eli.

"I'm as sure as your bad-sorta-fell-asleep driving."

They both laughed, high, and a little nervous, as they approached the door. Eliza rang the bell and they both stood back toward the edge of the stoop. She held her hands together in front of her like a schoolgirl. Eli had one arm around her shoulder, the other behind his back. They waited.

A woman they assumed was Ann-Marie answered the door. She did not at all fit the image of the people they had become used to working for. She was blond with loosely curled hair. She wore thick blue-framed glasses that called attention to what was already a prominent nose, sharp and pointy. Her short, tanned athletic legs, the green of her veins shining through the skin, holding up her petit, frumpy frame, gave off a soccer-mom vibe. Eliza wondered what Eli was thinking, and for a moment she imagined they were both expecting two chubby little kids to come running out from behind Ann-Marie, chasing out the smell of baked cookies.

The woman stuck out her hand to greet them. They reached for it at the same time. The woman grabbed Eli's, and then Eliza's.

"Hi, I'm Ann-Marie, nice to meet you. Come on in." She led them to the kitchen. "Would either of you like a drink? There's juice, milk, sodas, beer, gin, rum, or vodka. We want you to be comfortable."

Eli and Eliza replied in unison: "Just water." They all laughed, and relaxed a bit. They sat for a time in the kitchen chattering on as if they were at an afternoon barbecue with friends. Then Roy came in and the conversation stopped. The camera in his hand served as a reminder of why they were there.

"Hey, kids. You ready to get started?" asked Roy.

"As ready as we'll ever be," said Eli.

Ann-Marie stood behind Eliza, her hands on Eliza's shoulders. "Okay, darhlin, you follow me to the back room."

Eli wasn't letting go of Eliza's hand. He squeezed it. "Hey, guys, could we have a minute?"

Ann-Marie smiled. "Of course, you can just step out on the back porch for a little privacy, and perhaps a cigarette. You kids sure you wouldn't like a drink?"

Eli acquiesced and took a beer. Eliza followed his lead and asked for vodka and soda. Drinks in hand, they went to the front room. Eliza could see Ann-Marie and Roy in her periphery, Roy shaking his head. Ann-Marie had her fingers to her lips, her head tilted slightly to the side, signaling, Eliza believed, for her husband to give his temper tantrum a rest, and let them have a moment.

"Baby, you wanna leave?"

"No, I just don't want to fuck Roy."

"Come on, Eli. Jacob would've told us if it was that kind of situation. He's never led us in blind before."

"I know."

"So shake it off. Let's get in there and get our money. Baby, it's four hundred apiece."

"Baby, you got any more pills?" It came out slurred, a sign of sufficient escape from reality. Eliza dug into her pocket and handed him two hits of Adderall; it was time to get up.

"Where'd you get that?"

"Seriously? Just fucking take it." She slipped one into her mouth too, and washed it down with the vodka.

"You kids all right in there?" asked Ann-Marie.

They walked back into the kitchen, glanced at one another, and then headed off. Eliza, following Ann-Marie, looked back to see Eli as he stepped into the shadow of Roy and headed off toward the garage. She hoped Jacob hadn't left anything out.

Eliza walked into a pink pastel bedroom perfect for a twelve-year-old girl with a serious frills and teddy bear jones.

"Okay, doll, get naked," said Ann-Marie.

Eliza pulled a sea foam–green teddy out of her purse; she loved the way the color looked on her skin, and held it up. "Sure you wouldn't like me to start in something?"

Ann-Marie stared at the garment. "No, just naked and masturbating are all we'll need for this scene. It would be great if you could incorporate the teddy bears. There'll be no need to talk. You understand, right?"

Eliza put her lingerie away; this was about sex and not about her. The camera didn't need her memorable, just wet and ready. She got on the bed, tried to take herself to the moment when she and Eli were leaving the apartment, when fucking seemed like a natural reaction, but the thought of him was a reminder of how she got here. It stirred anger, not ecstasy. She felt empty. The deeper she dug, the harder she rubbed her clit, the harder she jammed her fingers into her pussy, the more she writhed, the tighter she squeezed her nipples, the less she felt. It went on like that, finger fucking, licking, and performing with teddy bears licking her ass for what felt like forever.

Ann-Marie's voice broke the tension of her heavy breathing. "Do you think you can come now? I know I could. Like a little help?"

Eliza looked from the camera into the willing, wanting eyes of the pornographer soccer-mom. She pressed into her clit, arched

her back as she laid into the stuffed animals, moaning and screaming. She faked her orgasm.

"That was fantastic. You can have a smoke, grab another
drink, get dressed or not, and go to the porch. We'll start the next
scene in a minute."

Eliza put on her shoes, nothing else, and walked into the
kitchen. Eli was tied up in the center of the large kitchen table.
His hands and legs were trussed up behind him with rough blond-
colored rope, silver duct tape over his mouth, and a red bandanna
covering his eyes. Roy smiling and directing him: "Move around
more, really struggle."

Eliza grabbed a cigarette from a pack on the counter, walked
outside, and lit up. She stared out at the pool. It reminded her of
home, her parents' house. She wanted to dive in. Swimming always made her feel free no matter what had happened to her inside
their house. Underwater she was silent, and safe. The tap on the
glass door startled her.

"You ready to go again?" said Ann-Marie.

Eliza nodded her head to indicate yes, crushed her cigarette in
the ashtray, and followed Ann-Marie back into the house. She always seemed to be following someone into something she'd rather
be walking away from. The day went on, one room to the next,
Ann-Marie leading the way to singular sex with vibrators, fingers, and remote-controlled fuck machines. The length and girth
of which had convinced Eliza that the in-and-out friction, the intense pounding of her now swollen vagina, was sure to decommis-
sion her ovaries or—at the very least—provide her with the gift of
a yeast infection.

Eliza and Eli saw each other one more time, both tired, him
marked with red welts, during a naked cigarette break by the pool.
A forty-five-minute eternity later, they left the house together, the
sky now inhabited by the moon. They walked slowly, quietly back

to the end of the drive eight hundred dollars heavier, and got into the car. In that silence, they quietly breathed their day in and out, Eli peering back over his shoulder every few minutes. Perhaps, Eliza thought, his furtive backward glances were to see if A & R, seeing them stationed there at the end of their drive, would be coming to ask them to do just one more scene. At the thought of it, she started the car and headed toward the highway. One hand on the steering wheel, the other digging for a cigarette in her purse.

"So, should I call Moses?"

Eli grabbed the mobile phone out of the glove compartment and dialed, smiling, revitalized at the thought of what they were moving toward.

"Hey, Moses, where are . . . ? We can be there in twenty . . . What do you mean, don't rush? You out . . . ? Oh, okay, we'll wait in the parking lot . . . What? Okay, okay."

"What'd he say?"

"He has to re-up. He doesn't want to see our faces any sooner than an hour from now. Fucker freaked out when I said we'd wait in the parking lot."

Eliza fumbled for a CD, looking between the CD case and the road. She shoved in the silver disk with *SONIC* written across it. The sound of Kim's sultry moan of a voice opening up Sonic Youth's "Teen Age Riot" filled the car:

> *Hey, you're really it*
> *You're it. No I mean it, you're it*
> *Say it, don't spray it*
> *Spirit desire (face me)*
> *Spirit desire (don't displace me) . . .*

Eliza turned the volume down before Thurston's voice could come crashing in. "Fuck it. He's going to find a reason to yell at us either way. We'll park at the edge of his lot and call the minute that obnoxious black, gold-trimmed Lexus pulls in. Don't look at me like a scared little kitten. I won't let Moses smack you up."

Eli smirked, settled back into his seat, and focused his gaze out the window. No doubt counting his chickens before they'd hatched, little dancing eggs of dope doing the conga in his head. His four hundred already spent.

Eliza killed the headlights as they pulled into the parking lot. They stationed themselves in a spot at the edge near the street, and she rolled down their windows. The night was warm and sticky, with no sign of a breeze swooping in to save them. She and Eli commenced chain-smoking cigarettes, their growing pile of butts at either side of the car—a definite trail to their destruction. They waited, occasionally remarking on something unrelated, like the fantasy that they'd get food before they booted up. Eliza called the bringer for the third time. No sign of the black car.

He finally answered. "My guy's not here yet. You two fucks better not be outside. Stop muthafuckin' ringin' me. I'll find you when it's time." The click of the phone slammed into her eardrums.

The heavily adorned Lexus—big black wheels sticking out too large for the body, soft yellow LED lights flickering inside the metallic spinning gold rims—rolled into the parking lot forty-five minutes later, Spoon's "Jonathon Fisk" pumping out of the windows in disjointed fits with reverberating bass:

Maybe you're locked away
Maybe we'll meet again some better day some better life
Jonathon Fisk speaks with his fists
Can't let me walk home on my own
And just like a knife down on my life . . .

The unlikely choice of music stopped abruptly. Eliza and Eli looked at each other holding back laughter, before ducking down in their seats, thinking the inhabitants of the car might have seen them. When no sound of footsteps materialized, they sat up just in time to see Moses strolling over to the black Lexus. The lights on the car dead, the inhabitants were now just three shadows, slapping hands and making small talk. The exchange must have been going on down low, in between the front and back seats. Moses got out of the car walking backward, waving and smiling. The moment the back end of the Lexus bumped up and over the curb, he was walking toward them.

"Fuck," punctuated Eli's last meandering sentence about ninety-nine-cent burritos at Taco Bell. They froze, their fingers twitching, legs mindlessly shaking at the sight of him, their savior; his lithe cocoa-brown shape walking toward their car, seemingly gliding in slow motion, his steady approach bringing the guarantee of having to patiently sit through a flow of venomous words to get what they wanted.

He didn't speak, just got in the backseat. They forced smiles to their faces, and handed him money too soon and without any finesse, as they attempted to exchange pleasantries: *How's your wife Sheila?* His wife-girlfriend in prison on a five-year drug traffic charge he had happily let her swallow after shoving his drugs in her purse. Their questions flowed out jumbled and too close together.

Moses shook his head and let out what they presumed was a laugh. "Fucking junkies." He never answered their questions, just handed them their bundles of powder and pocketed their money. "I shouldn't sell you shit. You've been fucking sitting here the whole time, even though I told you idiots to wait somewhere else."

They played dumb; their silence was an agreed-upon sign of respect—never wanting to upset him to the point that he might make his threats real.

"Next time you get nothing. Anyway, this shit is good so be

careful." The biblical bringer had spoken. He got out, slammed the door, and walked away.

"Where should we go?" Eliza asked.

"Anything with a bathroom or a parking lot."

"Let's go to Wendy's."

"Hawkeye Wendy's? Where that guy chased us out last time?"

"It's not like they posted our pictures on the fucking window."

They pulled into Wendy's, parked by the door, and headed with purpose to the back of the restaurant, checking behind them before entering the handicap bathroom.

"Hand me a bag and my spoon."

They looked at each other one more time, dueling syringes clasped between lips and teeth, the first part of the ritual complete. Needle in, blood out.

Calm. Then, her ears ringing, she dove into nothingness, didn't try to hold on. The first slap across her face was like a cool paper towel, the second shook her back into the moment. With Eli's face looming over her, his lips shaped into some sort of scream, she waited for sound to come back.

"Fuck! I thought you were dead."

"You crying?"

"Fuck off."

"That's the best shit we ever got from him."

They smiled collusively, Eliza cradled in Eli's arms. He wiped a dribble of spit from the corner of her mouth. She went to the sink to look at herself in the mirror, wash her face.

"I need a hit, baby. You're dying shit blew my high."

"Let's go back now before he runs out."

"I'll be quick."

"You take too long, I'll leave your cockroach ass."

Eli smacked her ass, then watched her smile disappear through the closing crack in the door.

Eliza was still listening to the phone ring when he came out walking on air. Fuck me if he isn't beautiful—her thought punctuated by Eli clutching his stomach and puking on the hood of the car. "Jesus Christ, Eli."

"This ain't fuckin' Eli," came the voice on the phone. "You know whose number you callin', bitch?"

"Sorry, sorry, it's me, Eliza. Is it all right if we come by?"

"You just left."

"Yeah."

"Don't get fresh. Yeah, come up." The phone went dead.

She pulled into the bringer's, and moved toward his place solo. She knocked on the door. The mess that greeted her was a mirror reflection.

"Fucking come in."

She walked in, Eli on her heels. "What the fuck!"

He smiled. "What, baby, you thought I was gonna sit in the car and leave you to your own devices?"

A calm, subdued PRDD slumped himself onto the couch.

"Hey, is it okay if I smoke?" The cigarette was already in her mouth, the match already headed for its end.

"Guess so."

Eli and Eliza sat on the maroon, gold-trimmed love seat, PRDD remained slumped on his matching couch. The place looked like a rent-a-center model home. An uncut pile of dope winked at them from atop a large mirror covering the coffee table; the mirror's edges a no-fly zone, its passenger too precious for the floor.

"We wanna get two hundred."

"Put the money on the counter. Get me a Ziploc."

Eli started to stumble to his feet, his hand reaching out to use the mirror for leverage.

"Sit down before you do something stupid."

Eliza, sure footed, headed to the kitchen, put the money on the breakfast nook. The idea grabbed her just as her fingers reached for the baggies.

"Hey, Moses, can I grab a beer? "

"What, I'm your hostess now? Just bring the fuckin' bags."

"All right."

"Nah, just kidding, bring me one too."

She unhesitatingly dropped two bars of Xanax into his beer.

"Thanks. Wanna line, chickie?"

"Nah, not unless you're gonna let me put that line in my arm."

"Whatever."

Eli's hand moved like lightning to his back pocket. She rolled it over in her head; one shot and both these cunts will be out. She took nothing and stirred it into her spoon, preparing to shoot ice-cold water in her veins.

"Baby, hold me."

Eliza grabbed the top of Eli's arm. He went in for a spot. PRDD's head sank toward the scattered two-foot line waiting for him. Eli was out. She'd deal with him later, right now she needed him out of the way for this to work. She sat back and waited. She watched the bringer's head resting on the back of the couch, mind gone. Then he came to, swallowed down half the beer.

"Moses, can we talk in the bedroom?"

"What?"

She smiled; nudged her head toward her drooling, dope-blessed seatmate.

"Oh yeah, yeah."

She grabbed the bringer by the arm, led him to his bedroom. He pushed her up against the door, roughed up her tits. She moaned, and she passed her hands along his limp cock. They moved toward the bed. He plopped onto the corner, hard mattress protruding from between his legs, his head sagging down. She waited a few seconds, then pushed him back, started to unzip his pants.

There was no need to take the charade any further; he was out.

She raced to the front room, grabbed a freezer bag, shoveled the drugs in, ran to the bathroom, took the lid off the tank, and seized the double-wide freezer bag of cash floating there. She roused Eli. "Come on, baby. Let's bounce."

"Where's the bringer?"

"Sleeping."

Eli didn't notice the extra baggage she was toting. She shuffled him down the stairs and into the car, not looking back once. They'd have to leave to wherever now, or they'd be dead by tomorrow. One stop. They needed to go to the apartment to get clothes, a quick in-and-out.

The car came to a screeching halt, half on the street, half on the walkway. "Wait here. I'll grab our things. Be right back."

"Where's our stash, baby?"

"Not now. We gotta leave."

"Why?"

"Don't ask."

"Come on, baby. I need it."

"Okay, let's go."

She'd miss him when he was gone. He was so beautiful. She watched him stumble into the bathroom with a ridiculous scoop of drugs in his paw; ritual. The door closed.

"I'll be waiting in the car when you're done."

Eliza walked out, got in the car, and headed for the highway.

At least he'd be high when the bringer came. She'd be high, too, in a couple of hours. On some beach figuring out what was next. Fuck, maybe rehab was in her future. There had to be something beyond this, there had to be a better way to live. She turned up DNA's "Not Moving" and let it screech through her speakers as she laughed and cried over the memory of the men she had just left behind; the looks that would be etched onto their faces when they finally came to.

NATHAN LARSON is best known as an award-winning film music composer, having created the scores for over thirty movies, including *Boys Don't Cry, Dirty Pretty Things,* and *Margin Call.* In the 1990s, he was lead guitarist for the influential prog-punk outfit Shudder to Think. He is the author of the novel *The Dewey Decimal System* and its sequel *The Nervous System.* Larson lives in Harlem, New York City, with his wife and son.

dos mac + the jones
by nathan larson

Dos Mac, accomplished urban planner and the mind behind some heavy-duty military technology, is draining his first cup of coffee as he notes an ancient but absolutely unmistakable tug in his groin and stomach.

Dos gives it a second. Player, please, he thinks. But there it is, that heat in his gut. If you've felt it once you couldn't possibly misdiagnose it.

Sets down his brown MTA mug on the metal gurney that now supports his piecemeal bachelor's kitchenette. "Motherfucker," says Dos into the stale air of his cavernous live/work laboratory.

How long had it been? Three years plus, but Dos knows this is irrelevant. The Jones is an eternal flame. The Jones is terminal. The Jones rides shotgun in your lizard brain toward the infinite night, its soft tendrils tickling your prostate. Into the grave, perhaps beyond.

Dos rocks an off-off-white Puma tracksuit, flip flops. Clothes he fled his apartment in, over six months ago, when they blew up the bridge nearby. Everything is outsized, he is shrinking, drying up. The loose flesh of a once stocky man hangs off him like a shitty suit. His hair is untended, or natural, or "nappy," shooting skyward from his scalp in a salt-and-pepper afro. He places his hand on his cheek, calculates the length of his beard to be just shy of a centimeter. A yellowed plastic breathing apparatus hangs loose around his neck, from which a thin tube dangles freely.

Dos Mac is not the name he was born with.

"Motherfucker," the man repeats. For there is no doubt as to what he must do.

He envisions his "day" with growing horror and annoyance. Plans for further microscopic tweaking of the 3-D model of the reconstructed subway system (which, admittedly, he has been tweaking for weeks on end) are now fucked. He would need his oxygen tank and hand cart. He would need . . .

Problems present themselves to the man, with respect to securing some heroin. Dos Mac has no idea what day or time it could possibly be. And more to the point: he has no idea where to look in New York City, his hometown rendered alien to him after the "attacks" of February 14, the island of Manhattan a decimated void, now in an endless state of rebuilding, seemingly leading nowhere, one massive semi-abandoned construction site. He has no clue as to who would have the good stuff on hand. Or if shaking some loose is even a remote possibility.

He shuffles sideways, turns a bit. Blinks at the wall of computer monitors, stacked willy-nilly, closed-circuit cameras showing Times Square, barren save a tractor, a couple NYPD vans, and a loose grouping of soldiers in black ninja suits. Another screen shows the corner of Hester and Broome, and forty feet east of that, yet another camera is trained on the sidewalk outside his front door, which is virtually traffic free.

The fluorescent light over the right-hand side of the rear of the gigantic room flickers. Once that goes, simply getting a bulb for the shit will be a serious, likely a very dangerous, task. And suddenly he has the fucking stones to fancy he can saunter out, pick up some smack, and be back before lunch? Dos Mac is kidding no one.

His regular NA posse would be disgusted with him. His sponsor would wobble his head at the staggering waste of it all. All that work. The breakthroughs and milestones, the weepy mea culpas and poker chips, all for naught.

But there is no more NA. Finito. No more meetings. The "rooms" sitting silent and derelict, or buried under rubble and ash. Either way, that crutch is history.

As addicts go, Dos had been more than highly functional. In this and in all things, the Mac excelled. Some labeled him an over-achiever, perhaps attempting to compensate for his bleak roots in the housing projects of Brownsville, Brooklyn. Dos found this insulting, simplistic. Everybody's got their scene. His scene was that he was black and poor in America, but damn, haven't we done away with the stereotypes and all that bullshit? Apparently not.

At what point do you stop being a prodigy? When you hit eighteen? At twelve? When is it no longer charming? At what juncture do you become just another annoying brain clogging the coffee shops and microbreweries near MIT?

The thing with Dos and the smack was never an issue of health or well-being. Nor did anybody aware of his habit do more than whine at him for being fucking lazy. Or for not sharing. Most of his trashy ex-boyfriends, with their nonstop waxing and bulimia, most of these trifling faggots he wouldn't wish on his most hated enemy.

No, the issue was money. As in, he spent it all on drugs and therefore had none. That was what got him, eventually.

At the absolute height of his game, Dos floated untouchable through space and time, his habit and his career tracking parallel, neither affecting the other in the slightest. He had a long good run: as a youngster Dos had fast-tracked it through Brooklyn Tech. By night, he mainlined and freebased it through as much junk as his body could handle. Somehow his sense of how much was too much was very finely honed, and Dos Mac made sure to stay on the right side of that line.

For all his scag consumption, Dos had always been a bit of a health nut, with an emphasis on the nut. No alcohol, no over-the-counter painkillers . . . plus, a strictly meat-, gluten-, and dairy-free diet. Even in these current conditions. And trust, this regime is not easy to maintain in the best of circumstances. Try keeping it up in a husk of a town like this one.

After his creation of the missile guidance system (originally conceived as an attempt to increase efficiency in the NYC subway), and Mac's subsequent courtship by the government, his stint in naval intelligence made maintaining his smack hobby a touch trickier. The pop drug-testing, the security screening. He's positive that brass willfully ignored some serious red flags. And although folks can get used to anything, it wasn't exactly comfortable, smuggling clean urine around the academy grounds, plastic test tube shoved up his ass.

Yeah, it was trickier in the navy; that is, until he got deployed to the Motherland. That depopulated hole, where the poppy fields grow wild and unchecked. Manna, in unending supply. Dos even toyed with the notion of investing in the thriving export operation, whose participants and actors were countless within the ranks of the military and private contractors. It seemed safe enough, but in the end, Dos, content in his role as a user, wanted only to get high and play with his models. He was no businessman and certainly not an enthusiastic risk-taker.

Now Dos Mac catches himself itching his arm, in anticipation. For a dude of extreme caution and calculation, what he's contemplating would have to count as one of the most reckless acts he's ever undertaken.

He'll have to go Out.

It's just that way, that's just the way it is. Damn.

How long, how long since he's been outside? He glances at his monitors again, anxiously, as if they might hold some crucial information. Weeks? A month? If anything has changed it will have been for the worse, that much is for sure. Fucked up as it all is.

Tells himself: one last time. It's been a stressful year, to say the least. Isn't a man entitled to a little relaxation, having survived what some might describe as an apocalypse? And having bounced back in fine style to boot . . .

Even so, he'll have to go Out.

Where will he even begin? It's sure to have all been shaken up. Have to start locally, hope it's easier than anticipated. Maybe he'll luck out. He'd never bought in Chinatown, but seeing as everything else has been turned on its head, Dos sees no reason why the drug market will be any different. Then he'll turn to spots he knew well and see what that might render.

He'll need goods to barter with. That's the way folks do now.

Dos dusts off a largish nylon sports bag, which bears the faded word *Modell's*. Tosses his desk drawers, not knowing what he's looking for. What do people need anymore?

Keys to the big locker—beside the hydroponic lighting, useless now as the plants have been dry and lifeless for ages (how did he allow that to happen?), here is his stock of premium items with which to barter: his seitan jerky, a couple cases of Fiji water, four Zippos, lighter fluid, several packs of rechargeable batteries, and the main event, a pair of Motorola Talkabout two-way radios. Dumps a sampling of everything into the bag, then pauses at the radios. This would be blowing his wad. Other than his generator, without which he would quickly find himself dead, these radios are the most valuable objects he has. The computer shit, the cameras, they'd be useless to most people. In giving up the radios he'd be severely limiting his options, in the likely event his generator fails.

At the moment, however, anything that might bring him closer to drugs must be put into play.

Extreme times, extreme measures, says the Jones, from behind his inner ear. It's the voice of his former sponsor, Charles Morgan, for reasons Dos doesn't care to explore, a voice island-tinged, disciplinarian, prone to faux-profundity and platitudes, probably to lay down cover for the workings of a simple mind.

Dos takes a long, truly loving gander at his lab, his cell, his womb, his asylum. The amount of sweat and effort he's put into making it safe, making it a proper workshop. February 14 was a blessing in this way; he'd never felt as secure anywhere else. So much of him is here. His plans, his model of the perfect subway system, with its flat-zero carbon footprint, a version of the jammie he'd set up in Washington, D.C., writ large . . .

If you love something, set it free, says the Jones, which apparently is going to persist uttering goofy clichés that don't even apply to the situation at hand.

Regardless, Dos figures, making a final scan of his improvised safe house, he has little choice but to set out, because sometimes a brother simply has got to get high.

That smack won't be coming to him. He'll have to go to the smack. He tosses the radios in with the rest of his crap, and shoulders the bag.

Outside.

The air, the air crackles and pops with toxins, chemicals, fumes. The air is visible, a permanent fog. It's gotten much worse, worse than even a month or two back. Dos sucks at his oxygen, glad for the mask. Behind his chunky glasses his eyes burn, tear up. Would def not want to wipe at them with his bare hands; he learned that lesson early on.

On the corner of Chrystie and Delancey he squats, blinking rapidly. Feeling that inner drug-tug in his stomach. Thinking, can't believe I'm actually doing this.

Thinking, goddamn, peep all this. It's *all* Chinese now.

It was nearly all Chinese prior to 2/14 anyway, but given their resilience, economic superiority, and their steady access to bodies/cheap labor, they seem to be doubly thriving in this new environment. Dos is well aware that the Chinese have been awarded a fair number of Reconstruction contracts. And with that seems to have come a new energy, a new confidence. A palpable sense of Chinese superiority cuts through the nasty fog. What limited bustle can be observed seems purposeful, competent.

Glances that Dos has had at evil-looking Chinese military units leave him humbled. Wouldn't want to come to those dudes' attention. So, in this sense, the impression that he is completely invisible is a positive thing.

There's a trickle of rickshaws, electric vans, and sporadic drifts of workers on foot. Nobody loiters or appears remotely shady, with the exception of himself, reckons Dos; so he wouldn't dare approach any of these folks. No uniform, no proper ID . . . Where are the hustlers, the freaks, the lesser criminals? It's a rhetorical question. If he understood the Chinese even a little, such human debris would not be exactly welcome.

Oh snap. With discomfort, Dos recalls the Chinese government's posture of zero tolerance regarding narcotics. Given that these various neighborhoods have been all but handed over to the dominant group's rule of law, this area is looking less and less score-friendly.

Rising to his feet, ridiculous in his gas mask and flip flops, Dos Mac figures he'll have to press on. Head north, into Christ knows what.

Stepping around an open manhole, he trudges up Chrystie, dragging his oxygen tank behind him, clanking and top heavy on its rickety cart.

Ludlow between Houston and Stanton.

Third Street at Avenue C.

Avenue B between 7th and 6th Streets.

The "laundry" on 7th Street between B and C.

Nothing but blank spaces, in some cases the entire façade having been cemented over if not removed wholesale.

Near the former site of the "laundry," a work crew crouches, uniform gray coveralls, silently engaged in some kind of mah-jongg–like game. Dos Mac is positively ignored. Which is a good thing.

Dos realizing he's reaching as far back as the late 1980s, which is fucking sad, and that by the second address his wanderings have become nothing more than a masturbatory nostalgia jag. The Jones doesn't mind. It seems to only intensify the thirst, as the muscle/body memory is as strong as the perfume of a former lover. He digs on it, digs the internal heat.

Dos doubles down on this, his righteous mission to score. He's strong enough to make it this far? Motherfucker, he's strong enough to complete this simple task. The tug in his sphincter is, if anything, amplified as he moves through this neighborhood.

Does a nigger have to go uptown? Never comfortable around the dealers in Harlem . . . not that he expected to find anybody still hustling. What's going on uptown? Maybe, just maybe, an abandoned lab, somebody looking to unload weight for which there is no longer a market . . . but Dos knows he's just pipe-dreaming. Anything worth anything has been stolen, swapped, or sold.

Here, just look at his sorry ass. Dos Mac should be a subject for derision, should be attracting gawkers despite the thin population. But not so; not a solitary soul registers his movements. Dos makes no attempt at stealth, but he gets the sense that he's resonating ghostly, shadelike.

Besides appearing pathetic, and besides the fact that he's aware that a low profile is what will keep him standing, Dos Mac starts to question his own solidity; is he simply being snubbed, or has he somehow slipped into another dimension of being? Some sort of high-level physics at play here? Is he less real than the tire on the flatbed pickup that slows to collect the group of men, not pausing as they chase the vehicle and haul themselves up and onto the back of the truck, disappearing into the dirty fog?

Even the past has long split the scene, nothing is remotely recognizable, and all is brutally clean. Near silent as well, with the exception of far-off construction sites to the north and south. To all appearances virtually every structure has been carved out, shaved, scrubbed free of any former identity, and converted to serve some new and strictly functional purpose, or no purpose at all.

As Dos approaches 11th Street between A and B to find the entire block of former tenements razed, and an ad hoc shanty town in its place, he gets his first fleeting view of what might possibly be children and females. He takes a tentative step onto 11th Street. Chinese army tents, some semipermanent-looking, hard-plastic structures. The lingering smell of cooking animal meat, causing his mouth to immediately fill with saliva. He reminds himself, suddenly ashamed and slightly nauseous, of his principles regarding matters dietary.

The hood of old is gone, figures Dos. Which suggests he bring this swing down memory lane to a close. Operate in the now. The surface of the city he once knew is forever altered, and Dos Mac has to accept this fact, move forward accordingly. Or perish.

By the time Dos reaches what was at one time known as Union Square, he has to admit that he had no idea that Chinatown had exploded so comprehensively.

All Chinese.

With the exception of a small but intense Ukrainian/Eastern European enclave Dos stumbled through as he moved west, at about Second Avenue and 9th Street. Vehicles and buildings with Cyrillic lettering could still be observed. The old buildings less molested than further east. Knots of white dudes tracked his passage, chattering rapidly amongst themselves, hair cut close, veins protruding. No women, no women at all. Bemuscled goons with tattooed necks and hands displayed shoulder-holstered Glocks over their wifebeaters and polo shirts. Another trio of thugs, leaning out of a small truck, wanted to be very sure Dos clocked their hypermodern automatic rifles. All of which radiated some Aryan Nation shit for Dos, who put his head down and scurried on . . . As much as his mission calls for improvisation, he wasn't about to start up a conversation with these killers, despite the fact that they appeared rather likely to be in possession of narcotics. And all the more likely to start taking shots at him just out of boredom, or to audition their fancy weaponry.

Otherwise? The Chinese, goddamn, those fuckers have the lock on like every little thing.

Those Eastern European yahoos were way far from welcoming, but it was the first and only time on the journey thus far that anyone appeared to actually notice him. To see him, to see him and let be known he has been seen.

Hunkered down at the intersection of 15th Street and Union Square East, Dos sees it. In this new paradigm, there is no space for a drug like heroin. Oh, he can dig it. Any substance that might render the user vulnerable is less than useless. Allow your attention to flag here, you're extending an invitation to be looted, hollowed out, and stripped for parts like an abandoned car.

No, manic clarity is called for, and not the chemically induced kind of clarity . . . Watching an industrial crane lift crates off the back of a semi in the middle of the former park, flanked by gas-masked gunmen in Port Authority uniforms.

This is meth-amp territory, if anything. Good for physical labor. But a substance which, at least in Dos Mac's estimation, is the narcotic equivalent of a panic attack.

Dos seeks to escape this colorless nightmare, if only for a matter of hours. Not gonna hassle anybody. This is all he's looking to get done. Merely a short hiatus in the daily grind. Tomorrow morning? He'll be back at his desk, primed to do God's work, hankerings sated and silenced.

"That's it, man," he whispers, itching at his beard. "That's all I'm doing, taking time out. To look after me."

Well shit: his goal is certainly not to make himself all the more viciously present in the manner of the coked and methed up.

Look left, right, and sideways. Downtown is a fucking bust.

No. Dos will have to continue north. North is where the major Reconstructions sites are, and that's where dealers will orbit should there be any.

Friendless, there's no one, figures Dos. I need a gun.

The thought takes him from behind, and comes complete with a plan. The thought stops him cold.

A hospital. Why had he not thought of this from the jump?

Get a gun, get to a hospital, jack the staff for whatever's on hand in the opiate family. Do it fast and easy, nobody need get hurt. Forget digging up a bag; that format would seem to be extinct.

Get a gun. Tougher than it might seem, given the prevalence of guns. Helpless as he is, Dos will have to ask somebody nice, who in turn will have to give him a weapon of his own free will. It won't be the Chinese, or the Ukrainians.

Unbidden, the Jones pontificates: *That which kills you only makes you s—*

"Shut the fuck up," says Dos out loud. "Trying to think."

No. If I want to get a gun with only a moderate amount of risk, only one man springs to mind. And a serious wild card of a motherfucker at that.

The Librarian. Damn. I gotta see the Librarian.

* * *

Approached from the west, past the gigantic flame pits of Bryant Park, the New York Public Library remains almost eerily intact.

Mac makes his way around the corner of 42nd Street and pauses within sight of the famous twin marble lions. He is exhausted. At this point he's so far north, there's no way he'll make it back downtown without running out of oxygen. He's not positive if this will make any difference, but it's a huge risk.

Nobody around. Pauses to listen . . . Beyond the general hubbub of the fires and the clanging due east, which Dos assumes to be construction at Grand Central, the streets are barren.

Up the exterior stairs, his oxygen tank lighter and lighter, bouncing along behind him . . . he tries the main doors, finds them open. Dos steps inside and takes a moment, his weak peepers calibrating to the gloom.

The Librarian, he didn't want to think about how he knew this cat. Sure, he wasn't a bad guy, but damn. Goes without saying, this is not a dude you want to sneak up on unannounced.

On the other hand, Dos would hate to wake the man up. That could be an even darker scenario.

The lesser of two. Mac clears his throat.

"Librarian!" he calls, voice cracked and arid. Bounces off the vaulted ceiling. "Librarian! Dos Mac here! I'm unarmed, brother, I come in peace!" Trying to keep his tone light. You never know how the Librarian will come at you.

Dos gets no response.

There's two conflicting knots in his intestines; one is related to fear, and one is all junk-lust. It's the latter that pushes him upward.

Nothing ventured, drones the Jones, and Dos shuts it down. Jesus, what bullshit.

Calls: "Coming upstairs!"

Tough to see much on the stairwell, so Dos takes it slow and easy. Hefts the near-empty tank so as to make less noise. His flip flops feeling insubstantial and wrong against the cold stone.

One flight, and Dos takes a moment. Out of shape, breathing ragged. What the fuck does he think he's doing? I mean, honestly? Despite his military credentials, he is an engineer, a technician, a brain. The brother at the party who faded into the background, the dude who spoke too quiet or too loud, his movements subtly wrong, nervous, the kid who could never bust anything smooth. The guy you didn't notice till he, inevitably, knocked something over. Dos always liked to say he was a lover, not a fighter, but he wasn't much of either really.

Abort, reckons the Mac. Fuck this. Takes a step backward, reversing himself down the stairs. Cut your losses, son. Feels vastly relieved, having made this decision.

Crack.

A flip-flopped foot has found some kind of shell, crushing it under his weight. Not like the Librarian, thinks Dos idly, to leave garbage lying around . . . the Librarian, who to put it mildly is a bit of a neat freak . . .

Wham, and Dos's head hits a stair, as his legs are cut out from under him. The cart and tank go tumbling, and he finds himself facedown in a frighteningly professional choke-hold.

Smells: latex, baby powder . . . alco-gel. No doubt.

"Hey, Librarian," he manages, panic percolating, hold it together now . . . "It's Dos, brother, it's Dos Mac here . . ."

Overhead lights come on with a deep clunk, and Dos is released. He sucks open air, his mouthpiece knocked aside, and is grateful for it. Pushes himself up to a sitting position.

The Librarian hangs over Dos, blocking the light like a shadow puppet. Sharp angles, that signature hat.

"Well I'll be goddamned."

It's a rusty sound, that voice, dried syrup, tinted with cigarettes and filtered by the surgical face mask the Librarian wears.

"Mister. Dos. Mac," he says, separating the words.

"That's me, son," answers Dos, hoping he sounds calmer than he feels.

Librarian saying, "Gotta ask you first. Have you been in contact with any livestock, any individual who might possibly be carrying a communicable disease, shit along those lines?"

Dos shakes his head negative.

The Librarian extends a rubber-gloved hand. "Okay then. My second question then: what's a downtown nigger like yourself doing up here in the nosebleed section?"

Dos accepts the man's paw, and is hauled to his feet.

Mask dangling from its chinstrap, the Librarian is frowning at the spine of a blue hardbound volume. He taps it and looks up at the stack in front of him, which is a couple of feet higher than the top of his hat, leaning crazy. Says, "You're not for real." Says, "Thought Dos Mac, the gentleman, is all about peace . . ."

Dos raises a shoulder, thinking this was most def a mistake. The Librarian could be working for anybody and everybody. He had thought the man was strictly on muscle jobs for the city, but he could very easily be doing the odd Chinese gig, in which case . . . but this was paranoia.

Librarian saying, "Intelligent motherfucker like you? I don't need to point out—huh, do I?—that the mere presence of a firearm in the home exponentially increases the chances of . . ." He falters, distracted by some tiny aspect of the book's binding. He shakes his head rapidly, pops a pill of some kind. As he turns to Dos, he is shifting his mask back into place over his mouth and nose. "I'm not putting a judgment thing on you, man. No sir. Everybody gotta look out for their own . . ."

Dos ducks his head, murmuring his agreement.

"I mean, shit," continues the Librarian, stripping off his gloves and producing a four-ounce bottle of hand sanitizer. "I don't even wanna know what you need it for. Just, let's leave it there." Squirt. Rubs his hands vigorously, grabs a new pair of gloves.

Feeling the compulsion to give him something, Dos is aware of himself saying, ". . . Folks know I got computers, com units, and whatnot down at my place, word is I better watch my back should people get ideas . . ." Thinking, if this man can't smell a bullshitter . . .

The Librarian, adjusting his glove, lifts a hand and sets an index finger against his masked lips.

"Yo. Hush, Mac, I got you. I don't wanna know about it and that's my word. Wanna just plant this seed, though, an alternative approach, check it. Rather than bringing some heavy gun energy into your castle. I talk to the DA, we set up a man or two down at your joint, discretion for sure . . . 'Scuse me, is that a no?"

Dos has been shaking his afro. Says, "Don't want to put you all out. Just, just the loaner, and I'm straight."

The Librarian scans him. Curious. His eyes glaze a touch, and snap to a point just over Dos's left shoulder.

Spooked, Dos throws a glance behind him. Books, space, darkness. Returns his attention to the Librarian, who is in fugue mode.

"Crop sprayer."

Dos swallows. "Don't follow, my man . . ."

"We used to do it like that in the sandbox. You know about that? Helicopter, nerve gas, just blanket spots, neighborhoods. You could do it with drones. Insurgents hiding out, yeah, you get them but this, this shit kills everything, so you get . . . you get everybody else too. Regardless . . ."

Dos knows about this practice but doesn't see the relevance. "What's that got to do with—"

"Chinese, Russians, Saudis, all doing it to each other on the island. Knock out the competition and all that. Say to themselves, damn, it'd be nice to have that Brooklyn Bridge contract those other folks got and all, something sweet, meaty. Chrysler Building, whatever. Do a flyover, spray 'em, then before their crew can get more live bodies in there, you take the site. That's the realness. You haven't seen this?"

The Librarian seems to want to have a conversation about this subject, Dos is thinking it's fucked up to be talking to somebody when you can't see their mouth. He can only say, "I don't get out much, man. Doesn't surprise me, I've just never seen it, I don't go anywhere. Keep my head down."

The Librarian is nodding, looking at him. Out of nowhere he drops an explosive laugh, loud in this huge space even through the surgical mask, which morphs into a dry coughing fit.

"Head down, yeah," says the man, recovering. "Well, brother, that can only be a good thing. All I'm trying to say is, watch for low-flying helicopters, and you spot one? Run. See, the way I figure it . . . and mind you, I try to stick with this plan myself . . . if you don't appear aligned with one crew or the other, you're less likely to get targeted. Word to the worldly wise. You dig?"

Dos is nodding.

"Yeah," the Librarian is looking around like he's misplaced something, "yeah, just keep your head down like you're doing, you'll be all right, baby. For all I know? You and me are the last . . . *educated* black men on this island. I need you around, Mac, need somebody I can talk to. So, hey, if you tell me you got people trying to creep up on you, you want to be able to defend yourself in your own *home*, I hear you and am happy to be of service . . . You know what's a motherfucking shame and a travesty is the fact that a man has to . . ."

He disappears behind a pile of books, into the semidarkness.

Continues talking quietly but Mac can't make out specifics.

This motherfucker, thinks Dos, this motherfucker is insane. I can make a break for the exit, should this go south. Throw my bag at him and move. In fact . . .

Dos takes two steps toward the doorway and the Librarian is in front of him, mask down again. Smiling crookedly. Eyes black, with greenish shards, whites bloodshot. He points his chin at a gun, flat on both gloved palms. Shrugs.

"This here," he says with a chuckle, placing one hand over the pistol, "is a CZ-99 semiauto. Fifteen-round mag. Not so different than what y'all must've been issued. Point and shoot. Easy like that."

Hands Dos the gun, butt first.

"I appreciate this, I really do, man," says Dos. The weapon has been gaffer taped, light but solid; Dos thinking, I really do hate guns. I jockeyed a desk, *I sat it out*, there's a reason why I walked the path I did. Even so. Unzips his bag and places the pistol, gingerly, inside.

"This is a loan; heard me, you'll get it back."

Waving this away, Librarian says, "Hell, I borrowed it myself. And I reckon the previous owner ain't exactly gonna miss it, nah mean?" Winks at Dos, then snaps his be-gloved fingers. "Reminds me." He digs in a jacket pocket and fishes out a laminated card. "You're gonna want one of these, kid."

It's one of those city-issued jobs, featuring only a barcode and the words, *JUSTICE DEPARTMENT, PROPERTY OF THE STATE OF NEW YORK*.

Seen these before. Carried by protected scavengers/freelancers, like the Librarian here. Who says now: "Take it. For real."

Dos is pretty positive he's already had his DNA replicated, somewhat standard government stuff, etc., etc. Hell. If he looked hard enough he'd find a clone of himself swanning around. So he's not about to get all precious about his genetic code; otherwise he wouldn't handle such an object.

Plus, he's anxious to bounce. So as it is, he accepts the card, sliding it into his sweat jacket pocket. "Thanks, brother. Again, I owe you large."

The Librarian bats this sentiment out of the air.

Silence descends on them like a saturated blanket. Dos nods and makes to move for the stairs—

The Librarian intercepts him, wagging his skull, still wearing that shattered smile, snatches Dos's upper arm, hands like talons, a dead man's hands, thinks Dos.

"Snipers," whispers the Librarian. "Snipers everywhere, Mac. What's more . . ."

Comes closer, Dos smells sweat, cigarettes, stomach acid, and a faint undercurrent of urine. We all probably smell something like that, he reckons, weird I can't smell myself.

The Librarian speaks, quieter still, out of the side of his mouth: "Don't know about cameras but this bitch is bugged. Can't speak freely. Walk directly out the front and do it quick fast. I'll straighten it all out with the boss, though, not to worry. Jah bless, Mac, you're my brother."

Dos gets a stinging slap on the shoulder, probably meant to be friendly, but he's already turning, and without a backward glance he speed walks out of there, dragging his tank and cart. His bag feeling far heavier already.

Parked under a nonworking streetlight on the northwest corner of First Avenue and 33rd Street, Dos Mac is lightheaded, his chest tight. His balls ache, his mouth is dry. The Jones has him. His oxygen tank, dead weight, lies abandoned somewhere near Herald Square.

His choice of the former NYU Medical Center is based on the

fact that he knew where it was—next to what very little remains of an older hospital, once called Bellevue, which has apparently been entirely demolished. Good fucking riddance, mulls Dos, who'd had the misfortune of being consigned to that institution years and years ago now, in the meaningless past.

Gets lucky in the sense that NYU is still up and running. No question, a private military-industrial joint now. Point of fact: the spot is jumping, here in the pumpkin dusk, UN, army, NYPD, unmarked vehicles coming and going. Dos even spots an old-school ambulance, lights on, no siren. Stenciling on its side reads, *CORNELL/NEW YORK HO*. Everything's worn, mismatched.

Choppers sail past every couple minutes, visible only by their floodlights overhead. An open pickup truck rolls by, packed with Chinese men shoulder to shoulder.

All things in moderation, rambles the Jones in his inner ear. *Old dog, new tricks . . .*

He can smell the proximity of the pharmaceuticals. They vibrate, rattle him on a cellular level. Drug radar erect, drug meter pinned. There are drugs and they lie within reach. He's come this far to be warmed by their honey-sweet light, and yet he finds himself afraid. For if he cannot get to them, he will freeze to death, from the inside.

Scratches at his beard, rough. If Dos didn't know better, he'd tell you he is suffering withdrawal symptoms. Impossible. Doesn't fucking make sense, but there it is. It hurts, Dos is beat, and longs to have this done with, to float into the delicious embrace of the medicine, one fucking way or another.

A bird in the hand, says the Jones, and his stomach quivers. Unzips the bag, unsteady on his haunches, withdraws the gun, trying to decide how and where to carry the damn thing, settling on the shallow pocket of his sweat jacket, which barely covers the weapon and necessitates that he hold it by the butt.

Pulls the hood on the jacket up over his unkempt hair.

Observes the sorry details of his position, this parody. An unlit New York City alcove, a weaponized junkie in a hooded tracksuit, resolute, ill intent, eyes on the prize. Not exactly a novel picture. Ghetto stuff, unbefitting a learned man like Dos Mac.

Funny I managed to avoid such a situation until this very moment. All that focus and energy wresting free of the near-inescapable, gravitational field of a black hole like Brownsville. Shit. What heights I've known. Relatively speaking. And yet here I am.

Corrects himself immediately; of course, I am not a lost user, not anymore, don't be a fucking clown . . . I am, simply, an adult human, having a crazy day, indulging a craving, and am I not entitled to a little break, some misbehavior, as disciplined as I am, as hard as I apply myself to my work?

Scrolls through the available options for the umpteenth time. In terms of approach, they're pretty limited. Not much to do but waltz right in there and get as scary as possible.

Dos figures if there's a move to make he'd better make it before he passes out. The traffic has abated to the point where it's just gotta be done.

Plenty of time for analysis and/or shame, logics Dos, after I secure some drugs.

It's just me, thinks Dos, stepping into the street, abandoning his bag. Bearing witness to my own debasement.

Hands jammed into his insubstantial pockets, eyes on a Humvee and an NYPD Volt, both of which seem to be unmanned. Dos heads straight across First Avenue, aiming himself at the hospital's main entrance. He doesn't feel scary.

The gun is half in and half out of his jacket, Dos thinking he might be rushing events, contemplates turning around, the borrowed pistol continuing to slip, Dos scrabbling at the thing, feeling the duct tape, the rubber grip, his fingers seeking a more solid purchase, sliding through the trigger guard . . .

Doesn't so much hear the burst as register the abrupt absence of sound, followed swiftly by a numbness in his left hip. He is then aware that there has been a gunshot of some kind, pivots slightly uptown as the Librarian's disembodied mug floats on by, sniggering, mumbling, *Snipers*. Of course, thinks Dos, of course, and he turns again to face the hospital, peripheral vision gone, scanning the rooftops and balconies for some sign of . . .

Trying to work out why he would be targeted, trying to understand the intent of the handful of soldiers and cops emerging from the hospital entry, apparently headed his way, apparently shouting things he cannot quite hear. Dos brings his left hand out of his pocket and notes with detached interest that it is warm and wet with blood, tucks in his chin to discover yet more blood, an alarming quantity of blood, and it occurs to him that someone must have been quite severely hurt, and if this is the case it might make his mission to score that much more difficult.

This is as far as he gets before that thought bubble pops, and Dos Mac wilts sideways, collapsing to the pocked tar of First Avenue.

". . . Anywhere from thirty and fifty, gunshot wound to the hip . . ."

Dos is ripped out of a fairly neutral stupor by excruciating shards of pain in his side, faintly detects his body lifted and borne aloft, the pain abates momentarily, only to come crashing back as he is dropped on a hard surface. His bladder empties into his pants, hand wrenched awkwardly back, a metallic ratchet . . . his eyes are open and he is looking at his left wrist, secured to a bar with a pair of handcuffs, the attached hand apparently having been dunked in cartoon-red paint.

"Flip him," instructs a female voice from somewhere in this

overly lit room, and the agony that accompanies this action causes him to pass out again, though it's his impression that he comes to within seconds. On his side, cool air caressing an ass cheek . . .

". . . in and out," the female is saying.

"Self-inflicted," chimes in somebody else.

"Obviously," says the lady. Irritated. "But we can't do civi's. You rolled him in here? Now roll him back out."

". . . ID says he's Class A."

"This fucking guy?"

"Gotta confirm it but that's what he was carrying."

The lady sighs audibly. "All right, then. But I want security."

"Of course."

"It is what it is, let's clean him up."

The room starts getting shifted around, a uniformed guy materializes all up in Dos's grill speaking far too loud, as if to a retarded child: "Sir, do you know why you're here?"

Vision clearing by drips and drabs, Dos registers the faux-concerned, acne-scarred face of a white soldier. Not finding this worth deep study, he rotates his head, taking in a standard hospital room, several folks attending to the business of prepping for surgery, an Asian girl in Winnie the Pooh scrubs leaning over him, hooking a heavy plastic sack to an overhead rung . . . a bag of liquid . . . a bag of . . .

A bag of morphine.

"Sir, *do you know why you're here?*" repeats the soldier, sounding further and further away.

Dos saying, "I surely do, son. I surely do."

And like a cadaverous Buddha, Dos Mac smiles with his whole body. Extends his right arm.

Francis Delia

Novelist, journalist, and screenwriter, JERRY STAHL is the author of six books, including *Permanent Midnight, Pain Killers,* and *I, Fatty.* Most recently, he wrote the HBO film, *Hemingway & Gellhorn.*

possible side effects
by jerry stahl

Bad Penny, She Always Turns Up. That was one of my most popular campaigns, back when the porn business was referred to as Adult Films, not "triple-X content." Not that I'm a porn guy. I'm not. Anymore. I'm the kind of writer you don't hear about. The guy who always wanted to be a writer—who read the backs of cereal boxes as a kid—dreamed of being Ernest Hemingway, then grew up and wrote the backs of boxes. You don't think about the people who write the side effect copy for Abilify or Olestra ads . . . It's not as easy as you think. You need to decide whether anal leakage goes best before or after suicidal thoughts and dry mouth . . . I take a ribbing from some of the guys (and gals) at the office—which, I have to admit, gets to me. They know I've been working on a novel, but it's been awhile. I guess I should also admit that the heroin helps with some of the shame I feel about writing this stuff. Or life in general. I'm not, like, a junkie-junkie. I use it, I don't let it use me. And I'm not going to lie, it helps. It's like, suddenly you have a mommy who loves you. You just have to keep paying her.

Not that life is bad—I'm making a living, and not a bad one, considering; when I got my MFA I thought for sure all I had to do was start writing stories and things would just kind of take care of themselves. I realize now that it probably wasn't smart to use my "craft" to make my living. "Don't use the same muscle you write fiction with to pay the rent," my professor and thesis advisor, Jo Bergy, advised. Of course I ignored her. I wanted to be a writer!

In New York! But gradually, as the years passed, the bar for what counted as writing got a little lower while the pay, occasionally, got a lot higher. Why is that? Why should I be paid more for vibrator copy than my searching and personal novella about growing up the son of a blind rabbi and his kleptomaniac adulteress wife in Signet, Ohio? Sure, I placed a few "chunks" of the book as short stories in the beginning. That's what made me think I could do it. Though why I thought the three free copies from *Party Ball* magazine, or the two hundred I got from *Prose for Shmoes*, out of Portland, was going to make a dent in my living expenses, I don't know. I had some encouraging correspondence from *The Believer*. But ultimately they ended up printing the letter of protest I wrote when they rejected my twenty-first submission. Again, the drugs helped. I feel a terrific sense of shame about my whole life situation. I see other people my age making big money doing memoirs, getting screenplay deals based on tweets, and here I am bouncing around from porn dog to New Media Guy to Uh-Oh Boy—industry lingo for Side Effects Specialists, a.k.a. Sessies.

And yes, just thinking about this, the knife-in-the-chest regret I feel at chances blown, assignments fucked up, books unwritten or written badly . . . public scenes (more than once involving knee-walking, twice on a plane) when I was, you know, more high than I thought I was, it all twists me up. On smack, sometimes, you feel so perfect, you just assume everything you do is perfect, too. And when you remember, and the remorse kicks in, it's like a razor-legged tarantula crawling upside down in your heart, cursing you in dirty Serbian for being a lame-ass dope fiend who blew every chance he ever had and ended up in the world of incontinence-wear and catheters. (Referred to, just between us girls, as "dump-lockers" and "caths.") Well, do a little heroin, and you can remember the good things. On smack, everything feels good. I would gladly slit my own throat, attend the funeral, and dig my own grave, if I could do it all on decent dope—and not have to actually cop it. As William Burroughs said, it's not the heroin that'll kill you, it's the lifestyle.

But we were talking about the good things! Reasons for me to like y-o-*me*.

Like, not to brag, it was my idea to refer to the discharge from the rectal area as "anal leakage," rather than actual "intestinal discharge." Which, technically (if not linguistically) speaking, are two different things. My thinking was—and I said this to Cliff and Chandra, the husband-wife team who took over the agency—my thinking was, bad as "anal leakage" is, at least it's vaguely familiar. Tires leak, faucets leak, it's round-the-house stuff, and we all have anuses. (Ani?) But discharge is never good. Try and think of one situation involving "discharge" from your body that is not kind of horrible. Perhaps, hearing about my life and "career," you think *they* sound pretty horrible. Or maybe you're thinking to yourself: okay, he has some problems, he's had a bumpy career path, but he doesn't seem like a heroin guy.

Exactly! It's no big deal! Everybody has their little rituals. Miles Dreek, the other Sessie, walks in with his raspberry cruller and chai tea every morning. When I come in, I have my own stations of the cross. I go to the men's room, cook up a shot in my favorite stall, grab coffee in my ironic Dilbert mug, and amble back to my cubicle where the latest batch of American maladies awaits. Today, for example, is Embarrassing Flaky Patches Day. I watch the moving drama the clients have already filmed, showing a nice white lady with other nice white people in a nice restaurant, and listen to her VO: *It was a weekend to relax with friends and family. But even here, there was no escaping it. It's called moderate to severe chronic plaque psoriasis. Once again, I had to deal with these embarrassing, flaky, painful red patches. It was time for a serious talk with my dermatologist.*

Here's where I roll up my sleeves. (Well, at least one of them—haha!) From a list of heinous side effects I start cobbling together the Authoritative-but-Friendly PSE (possible side effects) list. *HUMIRA can lower your ability to fight infections, including tuberculosis. Serious, sometimes fatal, events can occur, such as lymphoma or other types of cancer, blood, liver, and nervous system problems, serious allergic reactions, and new or worsening heart failure.*

I had me at cancer! Seriously. I don't care if bloody images of Satan bubble up on my flesh, I'd have to do heroin just to stop worrying about the lymphoma and heart failure I might get for taking this shit to get rid of them. But that's me. That's the dirty little secret of TV medicine spots. The people who write them wouldn't go near the stuff.

Of course, people will tell you heroin is bad. But let me tell you my experience. If you take it for a reason, and you just happen to have a reason every day, then it's not exactly addictive behavior. It's more like medicine. Or a special survival tool. For example, there may be a thought that crops up in your head. (We're only as sick as our secrets!) Like how, lately, I have this thing, whenever I see a pregnant woman, especially if she's, you know, exotically dimpled, or has a really great ass, where I just sort of see her in stirrups, giving birth, her sweaty thighs wide open, the doctor and nurses with their masks on, the doctor reaching in, up to the wrists. It's better if it's a female doctor, I don't know why; I'm not proud of any of this. Once there's the actual pulling out of some bloody placenta-covered screamer, I'm gone. But still I think about—this is really not cool, really not something I want to *think* I'm thinking about—but nonetheless, what I think about, almost against my will, is how her vaginal walls—for which the Brits have a singularly disgusting word—will just be gaping. I remember it from when my ex-wife gave birth to our son Mickey. (She left me, years ago;

last I heard she was running a preschool for upscale biters. Which is a syndrome now; Squibb R&D has some meds in development. But never mind. Kids' drugs take a little longer for the FDA to rubber stamp.) Anyway, I just picture the gape. As riveting as Animal Planet footage of boas dislocating their jaws to swallow an entire baby boar. (The same arousal, it goes without saying, does not apply during a caesarean; I'm not an animal.) But still . . . when my thoughts—how can I put this?—veer in this direction, some non-wholesome wouldn't-want-to-have-my-mind-read-in-front-of-a-room-full-of-friends-or-strangers direction, I need something to get rid of the thoughts. I need the heroin.

Worse than fantasies are memories. Which may, arguably, qualify as disguised fantasy. Didn't George Bernard Shaw say, "The only thing more painful than recollecting the things I did as a child are recalling things I did as an adult"? Or was that Cher?

I actually started writing in rehab. (My first one. I've been in eleven. Three in Arizona.) And it was awful. The writing, I mean. We were supposed to paint a portrait of ourselves in words. I still remember my first sentence. *I AM TAPIOCA TRAPPED IN ARMOR!* Followed by: *Little Lloyd* (that's my name; well, *Lloyd*, not Little Lloyd.) "Little Lloyd" has cowered continually, long into adulthood, at the memory of deeds perpetrated on his young unprotected self, scenes of unspeakable humiliation. Which—can somebody tell me why? Freudians? Melanie Kleiners? Anybody?—barge into my psyche at the most inopportune moments. Imagine a big-screen TV that turns on by itself and blasts Shame Porn to all your neighbors at four in the morning. Like, say, I'll be at a job interview, talking to some wing-tipped toad named Gromes about my special abilities recounting the consequences of ingesting Malvesta, a prescription adult onset acne pill (glandular swelling, discomfort in the forehead, bad breath, strange or disturbing dreams), when I am suddenly overcome with memories of my mother paddling around the house with her hands cupped under her large blue-veined breasts, blaring Dean Martin. *When the moon hits your eye like a big pizza pie, that's amore!* She's high-kicking while our mailman, a long-faced Greek with a nervous twitch, peers in the window. And Mom knows he's there. I'm three and a half, and waiting to get taken to kindergarten. Mom's supposed to drive me, but instead, she starts screaming, over the music: *Why don't you play?* Why don't I play? It makes me anxious. Should the mailman be looking in the window? Where is his other hand? What happened to his bag? Ahhhhhh . . . Not even four, and I already need a fix.

Well, that's it. After the *That's Amore* flashback, I'm cooked. Forget the job interview. I'm like Biff in *Death of a Salesman*, grabbing a fountain pen and running out of the office. Except I run straight to the bathroom and pull a syringe from my boot. Minutes later, before the needle is out—AHHHH, YESS-S-S-S-S-S-S, *thank you, Jesus!*—The Mommy-Tits-Amore-Mailman image furs and softens at the edges. Until—MMMMM, lemme just dab off this little kiss of blood—what began as horror morphs into suffused light, savaged memory softened by euphoria into benevolence, to some slightly disquieting, distant image . . . Mom is no longer doing a dirty can-can in the living room, entertaining a twitchy peeper in government issue . . . Now—*I love you, Ma, I really love you*—now her legs are simply floating up and down. My mind has been tucked into bed. A loving hand brushes my troubled little brow . . . Heroin's the cool-fingered loving caretaker I never had. I mean, everything's all right now . . . As if my memory's parked in the very last row of a flickering drive-in, with fog rolling in over all the cars up front . . . So even though I know what's on the screen, and I know it's bad—*Is that a knife going into Janet Leigh?*—it . . . just . . . does . . . not . . . matter. It's still nice. Really nice. Provided, that is, I don't pass out in the men's room, and they end up calling paramedics, and I wake up chained to the hospital bed. *Again*. In California they can arrest for you for tracks. Those fascists!

And now—oh God, no! *No!* Here comes another memory. STOP, PLEASE! Why does my own brain hate me? I'm picking my son up at preschool, and I'm early, and I've just copped, so I go in the boy's bathroom. And—NO NO NO NO—I come to—you never wake up on heroin, you just come to—to screams of, *Daddy, what's wrong!* See my little boy in his SpongBob SquarePants hat, his mouth a giant O. He's screaming, screaming, and—what's this?—my ratty jeans are already at my ankles and there's a needle in my arm and my boy's teachers and the principal of the preschool are hovering over me, like a circle of disapproving angels on the ceiling of the Sistine Chapel and—

And I hear myself, with my child looking on, like it's some kind of *Aw shucks* normal thing, saying, *Hey, could you guys just let me, y'know . . . Just give me a second here?* And in front of all of them, in front of my sweet, quivering-chinned son, I push down that plunger. And suddenly, everything's fine. Everything's awful, but everything's fine . . . My little boy's horrified coffee-brown eyes glisten with tears. *Goodbye little Mickey, goodbye . . .* My wife will get a call from Family Services. I'll be leaving now. In cuffs. I manage a little wave to Mickey, who gives me a private little wave back. In spite of everything. I'm still his daddy. For years afterward, I have to get high just to think about what I did that day to get high. But it's okay. Really. It's fine.

Heroin. Because, once you shed your dignity, everything's a little easier.

Where was I? (And yes, maybe the dope did diminish my capacity for linear thinking. So what?) When my boss moved to pharmaceuticals from "marital aids," I followed. (He insisted on the old-school term his father used: *marital aids*. Instead of the more contempo *sex toys*.) We'd been taken over by a conglomerate. I cut my teeth on Doc Johnson double dildos (for "ass-to-ass action like you've never dreamed of!") and Ben Wa Balls ("Ladies, no one has to know!"). Then it was up (or down) the ladder to men's magazines, romance mags, even a couple of *Cat Fancy* imitators. Starting in back-of-the-book "one inchers" for everything from Mighty Man trusses to Kitty Mittens to X-Ray Specs. (A big seller for more than fifty years.) When I tried the specs, and—naturally— they didn't work, my boss said, with no irony whatsoever, "We're selling a dream, Lloyd. Did you go to Catholic School?"

"Methoheeb," I told him.

"What's that, kid?"

"Half-Jewish, Half-Methodist, and my mom did a lot of speed."

"Lucky you," he said, "I was schooled by nuns. But when I put on those X-Ray Specs, I swear, I could see Sister Mary Theresa's fong-hair . . ."

Don't kid yourself, this is a serious, high-stakes business. To stay on top of the competition, you have to know what's out there. Like, just now, on the *Dylan Ratigan Show*—What great hair! Like a rockabilly gym teacher!—I caught this: *Life with Crohn's disease is a daily game of "What if . . . ?" What if I can't make it to . . .* Here the audio fades and there's a picture of a pretty middle-aged brunette looking anxiously across a tony restaurant at a ladies' room door . . . The subtext: *If you don't take this, you are going to paint your panties.*

Listen, I spent a lot of time watching daytime commercials. I had to. (Billie Holliday said she knew she was strung out when she started watching television. And she didn't even talk about *daytime!*) Back when it was still on, I'd try to sit through *Live with Regis and Kelly* without a bang of chiba. Knock yourself out, Jimmy-Jane. I couldn't make it past Regis's rouge without a second shot. At this point he looked like somebody who'd try and touch your child on a bus to New Jersey.

Is it any accident that so much of contempo TV ad content concerns . . . *accidents?* This is the prevailing mood. Look at the economy. Things are so bad, you don't need to have Crohn's disease to lose control. But worse than pants-shitting is public pants-shitting. Americans like to think of themselves as mud-holders. You don't see the Greatest Generation diapering up, do you? (Well, not only recently, anyway.)

Junkies may be obsessed with bathooms, but America's got them beat. So many cable-advertised products involve human waste, you imagine the audience sitting at home, eating no-fat potato chips on a pile of their own secretions. As *Ad Week* put it on a recent cover, "American Business Is in the Toilet."

Right now, the real big gun in the Bodily Function sweepstakes is Depends. Go ahead and laugh. These guys are genius. Why? I'll tell you. *Because they make the Bad Thing okay.* (Just like heroin!) Listen: *Incontinence doesn't have to limit you. It all starts with finding the right fit and protection. The fact is, you can manage it so you can feel like yourself again.* (Oddly, I used to lose bowel control after I copped. May as well tell you. I'd get so excited, it just happened. So I'm no stranger to "mampers," as we say in the industry. They could ask me for a testimonial. Though, in all honesty, if it were my campaign I'd have gone with something more macho. Something, call me crazy, patriotic. *Depends. Because this is America, damnit!)*

Then again, maybe the macho thing is wrong. Maybe—I'm just spitballing here—maybe you make it more of a convenience thing. Or—wait, wait!—more *Morning in America*-ish, more Reagany. Take two: *America, we know you're busy. And you don't always have time to pull over and find somewhere convenient to do your business. With new Depends, you can go where you are—and keep on going. Depends—because you've earned it.* Subtext, of course: *We're Americans! We can shit wherever we want!*

See what I mean about dope making you more creative?

Not that I can mock. Ironically, because of my own decade-and-a-half imbibing kiestered Mexican tar, I got some kind of heinous, indestructible parasites. Souvenir of Los Angeles smackdom. For a while I had a job in downtown LA, five minutes from Pico-Union, where twelve-year-old 18th Street bangers kept the stuff in balloons in their mouths. You'd give them cash, then put the balloons in *your* mouth. If you put them in your pockets, the UCs would roll up and arrest you before the spit was dry. Keeping it in your mouth was safer. Unhygienic (parasites!), but on the plus side—visit any LA junkie pad, and there was always something festive about the little pieces of red, blue, green, and yellow balloons all over the place. Like somebody'd thrown a child's birthday party in hell, and never cleaned up.

But now—call it Narco-Karma—I have to give myself coffee enemas every day. Part of the "protocol" my homeopath, Bobbi, herself in recovery, has put me on for the Parasite Situation. Bobbi also does my colonics . . . She likes calypso music, which I find a little unsettling. Though Robert Mitchum singing "Coconut Water" while I'm buns-up and tubed is the least of my issues. Bob knew his calypso.

Like I say, part of my job is recon. And, I'm not going to lie, just thinking about that killer Crohn's copy makes me a little jealous. The subject, after all, was shame. What does some pharma-hired disease jockey know about *shame*? Did he have *my* mother? Scooping his stainy underpants out of the hamper and waggling them in *his* face, screaming she was going to hang them on the line for all his friends to see? (No, that's not why I do heroin. Or why I ended up in side effects. Whatever doesn't kill us just makes *us*.)

For one semester, I attended the School of Visual Arts in New

York City. I studied advertising with Joe Sacco, whose "Stronger than Dirt" campaign, arguably, sheathed a proto–Aryan Superiority sensibility under the genial façade of Arthurian legend. (For you youngsters, the ad featured a knight riding into a dirty kitchen on a white steed.) White Power might as well have been embossed on the filth-fighter's T-shirt. See—excuse me while I scratch my nose—there's a connection, in the White American subconscious, between Aryan superiority and cleanliness. "Clean genes," as Himmler used to say. Tune into MSNBC *Lockup* some weekend, when the network trades in the faux-progressive programming for prison porn. Half the shot-callers in Quentin look like Mr. Clean: shaved head and muscles that could really hold a race-traitor down. Lots of dope in prison. But—big surprise—the fave sponsors of *Lockup* viewers, to judge by the ads, are Extenze (penis size); Uromed (urinary infection); our old friend Depends (bowel control); and Flomax (frequent peeing.) The Founding Fathers would be proud.

You think junkies don't have a conscience? All the snappy patter I've cranked out, and you know what made me really feel bad? Feel the worst? Gold coin copy. People are so dumb when they buy gold—a hedge against the collapse of world markets!—they think it matters if it comes in a commemorative coin. A genuine recreation of an authentic 18-Something-Something mint issue Civil War coin with our nation's greatest president, Abraham Lincoln, on one side, and the thirty-three-star Union flag on the other. Worth fifty "dollar gold." *Yours for only* $9.99. The "dollar gold" was my idea. I don't even know why. I just knew it sounded more important than "dollars." Later, in the running text under the screen (known as *flash text* in the biz), I deliberately misspelled gold as *genuine multikarat pure god*. I think this was my best move. Not that I can take credit. Just one of those serendipitous bonbons you get when you type on heroin. This happened when I did too much. In an effort not to fall off my chair, I'd type with one eye closed. As if I were trying to aim my fingers, the way I aimed my car, squinting one-eyed over the wheel to stay between the white lines.

So now, now, now, now, now, what do I *do?* I mean—shut up, okay?—I did leave out a key detail. Like, how it all ended?

Okay. Let me come clean. (So to speak.) I got caught shooting up on the job. Dropped my syringe and it rolled leeward into the stall beside me, where my archrival, Miles Dreek (can a name get more Dickensian?) found it. And, long story short, ratted me out. I couldn't even plead diabetes, because the rig was full of blood, and everybody's seen enough bad junkie movies to know how the syringe fills up with blood. (Generally, on film, in roseate slo-mo, Dawn of the Galaxy Exploding Nebulae-adjacent Scarlet, which—come on, buddy—does not happen when Gramps drops trou and Grandma slaps his leathery butt cheek and sticks in the insulin. That was my first experience of needles: Grandma spanking Grandpa and jabbing the rig in. Grandpa had it down. The second his wife of his sixty-seven years geezed him, he'd pop a butterscotch Life Saver and crunch. Hard candy! Sugar and insulin at the same time. A diabetic speedball. *These are my people!*)

But wait—I was just getting busted. At work. (People think only alcohol can give you blackouts. But heroin? Guess what, Lou Reed wannabe. Sometimes I think I'm still in one . . .)

I remember, right before the needle-dropping incident, I was just sitting there, on the toilet, with a spike in my arm. Suddenly I jerked awake, feeling like one of those warehouse-raised chickens, the kind photographed by secret camera in *Food, Inc.*, on some infernal industrial farm, feet grafted to the cage, shitting on the chicken below as the chicken above shits on them.

You don't think they should give chickens heroin? Don't think they deserve it? Well, call me visionary, if they're already pumping the poultry full of antibiotics and breast-building hormones (rendering, they say, half the chicken-eating male population of America estrogen-heavy, sterile, and sporadically man-papped), then why not lace the white meat with hard narcotics? *Chicken McJunkets!* Whatever. Give me one night and three bags and I'll Don Draper a better name . . . Or I would, if I had a place to live. Right now I have enough to stay at this hotel, the Grandee (an SRO), for a couple more weeks. After that I don't know . . . Guy behind the cage in the lobby looks liver-yellow. Doesn't talk much. But never mind, never mind . . . Me being here has nothing to do with heroin. Just bad luck. But weren't we talking about heroin chicken? Believe me, plenty of clean-living junkies would hit the drive-through—provided Mickey D's could take those other damn drugs out of his birds. Hormones, antibiotics, beak-mite repellent . . . No thanks! That stuff could kill you.

Don't worry. I won't be out of the business for long. I have a plan. A new campaign. Look: Camera pans a modest but nice house. Outside, a sweet LITTLE BOY swings on a swing. Stressed-but-pleasant-looking MOM looks on, wiping her brow. *Mommy, watch!* yells the boy. *I'm watching,* says the pretty-but-tired woman, casting glances back toward the second-floor window. In which—REVERSE—we see our GUY peering out. We push in on him. He looks down at a foreclosure notice in his hand, then back out at the scene in the yard. His face registers complicated feelings: pain, regret, sadness . . . But we know what he wants. He wants relief. The man sits down on the bed, pulls out his works, and prepares a shot. We hear, in V.O.: *When I have emotions I don't like, I take heroin* . . . CUT TO: Man and wife together, in front of the swings. The man has his arm around the woman. The boy's beaming.

    Heroin. It makes everything good . . .

PART II

SURRENDER TO THE VOID

Scott Gillis

L.Z. HANSEN came to New York City in the early 1980s at seventeen years old, from London, England. She lived in the Chelsea Hotel and Hell's Kitchen before eventually settling in the East Village. Hansen has worked as a hair and makeup stylist, clothing store owner, streetwalker, speedball addict, escort, massage parlor owner, writer, and madam. She has been published in various magazines and anthologies, has spoken at colleges on her life and writing, and is working on her first novel. Hansen hosts her own monthly reading series, and enjoys life in the East Village, where she resides with her family.

going down
by l.z. hansen

Streets were hot, stinking hot. Sticky cans and discarded food collected around full garbage cans, and the flies were feasting. I felt cold. Goose bumps stood out on my arms. I noticed blood spots on the sleeve of my white long-sleeved shirt. I rolled them up just enough to hide the blood while still covering the pit of my elbow.

Sweat trickled down my back, and made me squirm.

A banged-up undercover cop car crawled past. The windows were rolled down, and two fat cops were sucking air. I slowed down and stood under a torn awning so they wouldn't see me.

One of them was the bastard who stopped me two nights ago on Rivington. On the street they called him Flash. I didn't know if it was in reference to Flash the superhero or the Queen song. I hadn't copped yet, but Flash swore he'd seen me score. He pulled me into a stairwell to pat me down. I knew he wasn't allowed, but there was nothing I could do. I was lucky he didn't plant something, and take me in. It's best to let the cops do whatever they are going to do. He felt me up, and stuck his hands down my pants. I think he wanted me to resist. The fact that I didn't pissed him off, and he told me to fuck off.

"Mama, youse looking for the good shit?" A man with one eye and one leg steadied himself against the wall. He smiled a toothless grin.

"No. Leave me alone." I said. The man's face stayed with me.

One eye, one leg, and no teeth. I wondered what else he had lost. If I had one eye I'd wear a patch. Don't see too many girls with an eye patch.

Walk down Avenue C. It's so quiet, and still daytime. The fiends weren't fiending, yet.

Houston Street. I saw a young hip-hop kid selling Road Runner by the Parkside Lounge.

Butterflies flipped in my gut as I neared the buzzing block. The seller was wearing a lot of gold, and stood out too much. I had five hundred dollars on me, which when transferred into dope, should have been enough to get me through the weekend, but it never did. It's never enough. Money had lost all meaning to me. It had become various amounts of heroin. My new currency. A hundred bucks meant a bundle; fifty, half a bundle; ten bucks, a bag; five bucks, a pack of smokes, not enough for a bag, and therefore meaningless. An annoying little piece of paper, unless accompanied by another five dollars, which had meaning, a whole bag of heroin.

A haggard street hooker stood in front of me in the dope line, and bought one bag. A nice-looking rock dude, the type I liked, pushed in front of me.

"Yo, da lady waz in front of youse," the dealer said.

Rock dude looked at me with hollow eyes and stepped back. Shame, looked like a cool guy, minus the dope.

"How many, Mama?"

"Five bundles."

"I got youse, I got youse . . ." He smiled flirtatiously. Then reached into his underwear and pulled out five bundles, tightly wrapped in rubber bands. I traded, money for heroin.

Beautiful. All's okay with the world. Now nothing could go wrong today. I felt my security blanket surround me.

"Thanks. Will you be here later?" Don't know why I said that, but I always did.

Walk quickly, quickly. Get off the block, off the block. Don't want to get stopped by the cops now. Hands deep in pockets, holding my life line.

It felt so good to have dope on me. It was the only time in my day that I could slow down, and view the world I had long ago stepped out of. The sky, the blue-blue cloudless sky, the people, feelings. I felt powerful and . . . safe at that moment. No one could touch me.

Then a large sweaty man appeared out of nowhere.

"Lady, please, you got a few dollars? I gotta get straight."

"Err . . . Hell no!" I looked at him like he was insane. I got mine, fuck him. Why would I give money away? That's bullshit. I felt guilty at being so cold and mean, but everyone for themselves, right?

I looked back, and saw him watching me. He made me nervous, and broke my momentary blissful view of the real world. I was bought back into my universe.

I saw Marilyn walking with a young, thin Hispanic male I didn't recognize.

"Marilyn!" I yelled.

Thank God, perfect timing. I could go over to her pad to get straight, instead of using the filthy bathroom at Odessa Restaurant.

"Can I use your place?" She knew what I meant.

"I was going to Tito's, you can get straight there. Got a bag for me?" she said smiling, linking arms.

Tito walked ahead, not talking. He took his T-shirt off and mopped his brow with it. He had a rough jailhouse tattoo of Jesus crying on the cross in the middle of his back.

I trusted Marilyn. She had been out on these streets her entire life, and knew everyone. Every dealer, hustler, whore, and thief.

In this life of disease, Marilyn was a beam of sunshine. She was always smiling. Even though she had little to smile about. She whored on Allen Street for ten bucks a pop and told me horrific tales of her life of abuse. Her ability to forgive and forget was astounding, and unusual. She had asked me why I spoke with an accent. I told her I was from London, England. She asked where that was, and if they spoke a different language there.

We headed to 3rd Street between Avenues C and D. The south side of the street was an open lot, where a building used to be. It burned down. Now, children played on strewn rubble and junkies turned tricks on discarded mattresses.

Tito pushed open the front door to the building. The lock was broken, and the hall stunk of piss and garbage. He angrily kicked an empty can of beer down the hall. It rattled into a corner and made me jump. Did he really have to do that? Asshole.

It was dark, the lightbulb was blown. We followed him to the second floor, to the back apartment.

Graffiti, newspapers, scattered bits of broken everything were everywhere. A young man was standing in a corner stooped over, on the nod, with an unlit cigarette in one hand and a lighter in the other. He looked frozen.

"Wake up!" Tito bellowed in the man's face. The guy opened one eye, smiled a crooked grin, and went back to his dreams.

Tito banged loudly, and put his ear against the door.

It clicked open and we all filed in past Tito's mother. She said she was going out to the liquor store.

How did people live in these filthy cramped places?

A sink was overfilled with plates and flies. Two shirtless men, one younger than the other, smoked crack at the kitchen table, filling the air with a sickly sweet smell. I held my breath.

"Yo, my man, Jojo? You gotta leave, dude. My mama needs you outta here," Tito said.

"She cool, I gave her money to go get two forties. I ain't leaving right now anyways. I gotta get me some more rock," Jojo replied.

"Yo, you can't sit here all motherfuckin' day . . . You been here two days, motherfucker, give me some more money then . . . nigga."

"I already give you fifty yesterday, fifty last night, motherfucker . . . Fuck you, T."

I followed Marilyn to the bathroom, passing Jojo, who eyed me up and down, licking his shiny lips. He was dripping in sweat, and his eyes were black and crazed. He made me nervous. I had to get straight, then get out of there fast.

"Where you find the white girl? Damn, I need me some white bitch . . . She got money, T?"

"Shut the fuck up . . . hell if I know . . ."

I heard them talk back and forth about me as though I wasn't there. I locked us in the small bathroom. I'd be quick. Gotta get straight.

I took the toilet seat. Marilyn took the edge of the bathtub. We quickly set up. I could do this blindfolded.

I wondered how many times I had stuck a needle in my arm . . . in my whole life? I shoulda kept a record.

I handed Marilyn a bag. She smiled and thanked me.

"What if the world runs out of water . . . ?" Marilyn asked.

"Huh?" Marilyn often came up with these bizarre paranoid thoughts.

"What if there's no more water on the earth, then what?" she asked, drawing up from a leaking bathtub tap.

"Don't worry about it," I said, annoyed, tying my arm with a shoelace.

"I mean, if there's no water, how are we gonna get high?"

"What?" I'd gone through this with her last week. "Babe, ain't never gonna happen . . . Look at the ocean, for God's sake, there's enough water for the whole world of heroin addicts to shoot up with."

"You sure 'bout that."

"Swear."

"Ain't it salty?"

Motherfuck!

"Think of all the rivers then . . . Babe, of all the things to worry about, that isn't something you should think about . . . really!"

Thankfully, she shut up for a minute.

Marilyn skin-popped because she'd long ago lost every vein in her body. She had large gouged-out craters all over her limbs, where she'd stuck herself a billion times. Once I'd watched her try to fix in the artery in the middle of her forehead.

The dope had already hit her, and she was feeling good, and beginning to ramble. Nothing worse than a fucking dope fiend feeling good when you're still trying to find a vein.

"Motherfuck. I fucking hate this fuck shit, fuck. My life is HELL!" I spat out furiously, as I tied up my other arm.

Sweat poured off my face. I was soaking wet. So was Marilyn. Still she smiled.

I couldn't get a hit. It was hotter than the devil's bedroom, and I couldn't breath. Sweat trickled into my eyes. I wanted to cry, but was too angry.

Blood dripped onto the floor. I marveled at how perfectly round and dark the drops were.

I heard Tito arguing outside the door.

I was so frustrated at repeatedly sticking myself; my works were filled with blood, and I didn't want them to clog. I finally asked Marilyn to hit me.

She grabbed my left arm, twisted it around, and squeezed. A decent vein I'd never seen appeared. She jabbed the needle in with one hand, while holding my arm tight with the other.

"You should have been a nurse," I said, as dark blood registered.

"Shoulda coulda . . ." She smiled.

I tasted the heroin. Warmth. Comfort. Relief.

At that moment, I loved Marilyn. Love. All's okay. *I really must control my anger.*

"There ya go." She pulled the spike out, and pressed her thumb to the spot that dripped blood. Her nails were dirty.

Nice. Not bad shit for Road Runner. *Don't know why I get so pissed anyway.*

We heard a loud crash and a scuffle. Jojo was threatening to burn the place up and kill me and Marilyn. Tito was yelling to get the fuck out, but Jojo said he needed money. Something smashed against a wall.

Marilyn and I locked eyes. She motioned to get into the bathtub. We did, and closed the shower curtains, quietly. Not that this was doing any good. We couldn't disappear and they knew we were in there. I thought Marilyn believed if she closed her eyes, no one else could see her.

Adrenaline and fear ruined my high.

We waited for something.

I was wondering how I got into these situations. I began making a deal with God that if I got out of this jam, I'd think about making some changes. Stupid negotiations I'd made with my God many times before . . . but somehow He'd always listened, long after I'd given up on myself. I seemed to live in someone else's life—how did my world become so . . . abstract?

"It's Jojo. He crazy, that crack shit turns him into el diablo, he with the Kings, he OG." Marilyn put her finger to her mouth listening. "Oh shit, he wants Tito to give him more money."

"Why? Tito has money?" I asked.

"No, he ain't got shit."

I prayed that the door to the bathroom wouldn't fly open.

"What does he want?" I whispered. My mouth was dry, I needed water, badly.

"Dope, money, what else is there?" Yeah, what else is there?

I looked at the peeling ceiling . . . and the tap that was leaking down Marilyn's back . . . Who cleans this place? Soap scum ringed the tub . . . my arm still hurt.

I needed a cigarette . . . always needed something.

The door to the bathroom suddenly blew open. I was terrified. The shower curtain was torn down. Jojo's face was deranged, a vein in his forehead looked swollen and about to burst.

"Get out. Get the fuck outta the fucking room NOW!" he yelled.

"Oh no, Jojo, don't do this," Marilyn begged.

"Where the dope?" he demanded, staring at me. "I know you got it."

He grabbed me by my hair, twisted it around his hand, and stuck a kitchen carving knife under my chin. The point pressed into my jaw bone, forcing my head upward. Jojo whispered between clenched teeth. His breath stunk like monkey balls, and he spit saliva onto my cheek with each word. I squinted my eyes, breathing through my mouth. His eyes were black and manic. His lower jaw jutted from side to side in spasms. His face and shoulders were twitching and jumping. He'd obviously been up for days smoking crack.

Jojo yanked me out of the tub and pulled me into the kitchen, ordering Marilyn to walk in front of us. He referred to the younger guy as D, who was holding a gun to Tito's head.

D then put the gun in the middle of Tito's back and walked him into the back room.

Tito yelled: "Jojo, I can't believe you, man, how long I know you, motherfucker, how long I known you? Damn, nigga . . ."

"It ain't personal . . . Shut the fuck up anyways!" Jojo screeched.

I jerked my head back and the point of the knife slipped and cut me under my chin. Blood dripped onto my white shirt. I felt the wetness run down my chest.

Jojo put his face into my hair and inhaled. He whispered, "I'm gonna fuck you, white bitch . . . but first you gonna suck my dick. I gonna fuck your tight ass . . . You like my dick, you gonna like me fucking your ass . . . ain't you?"

I held my breath as he talked. His teeth were stained and crooked. He pressed my hand on his crotch, which felt limp. His heart was thumping so hard, he was racing. There was no way he was going to get a hard-on. Sweat ran down the side of his face.

"Come on, touch it, touch it . . ." He opened his zipper. I looked straight at him and yanked on his soft sweaty dick. Way too much coke.

He leaned into me and rammed his tongue into my mouth, slobbering all over my face. His tongue searching my mouth, I tried not to gag, and left my body. Then, suddenly, as though re-membering what he was meant to be doing, he got up with his pants still open and screamed, "Give me the fucking dope! I know you got dope, bitch." He looked in my eyes. "We can party to-gether . . . I can get some rock . . . Yo, you like to smoke?"

My good God, was he serious? This had gone from a possible assault/rape/robbery to a fucking date. I knew my only way out of there was to stay calm and pretend I liked him.

"Yes, I like to smoke, of course I do . . . Papi." I giggled flirta-tiously. I tossed my hair back and stuck my tits out. "Here's the dope, Papi." I wanted to hold onto as much as possible. Noth-ing hurt worse than losing drugs. I passed him the two bundles stashed in my right boot. Maybe the dope would mellow him out a bit and he'd let us go.

He put the knife down, tore open a bag, and snorted it. Then another. Robbing us was like shooting dead fish in a barrel. What were we going to do? Yell for help? I just wanted to get the hell out of this place immediately.

I looked at Marilyn, who was standing wide-eyed and nervous. We heard Tito shouting from the back room, talking in English and half Spanish. D was asking Tito where he kept his money.

It got louder. Marilyn pleaded with Jojo to let us go. Jojo grabbed the knife that he had placed on the table and stormed into the back room, knocking over a kitchen chair.

I glanced at Marilyn, then the door, then Marilyn. Those few seconds seemed to tick in slow motion. Can we make it out of the door and down the street without them catching us?

We both leaped up and darted toward the front door, which had all sorts of bolts and locks on it. I slid the deadbolt, and pulled the door. It didn't open. I was never so terrified, my fingers trembled, Marilyn was banging me on my shoulder. I felt I was in one of those nightmares where I'm trying to run from someone, and my feet are stuck in quicksand.

"Come on . . . Mama, come on . . . hurry," she whispered.

"What the fuck do you think I'm doing?" I fumbled with two other locks, just yanking at them all. It opened! We both tripped over each other racing down the hall. Marilyn was practically on my back. I grabbed the staircase banister and flew, and I mean *flew*, down three stairs at a time . . . when we heard an extremely loud POP . . . from upstairs. Marilyn screamed. The gun? I couldn't believe it . . . I was running on the basic human reflex to save my life. Were they coming after us?

"Oh nooo . . . Dios mio . . . Dios mio!" Marilyn started yelling as we ran down the hall to the front door.

"Shut up, shush," I said. Two kids were sitting on the front stoop. We jumped through them onto the hot sidewalk that we had been on just twenty minutes ago.

The blistering sun, never-ending heat. I squinted my eyes to the blinding light. Marilyn says to *walk calmly, like nothing's unusual.* Whatever that means. We slowed down to a fast walk.

"What the hell . . . You know, that must have been D who fired that shot. I hope Tito's okay."

My mind was racing. I had to get some water. The thought of Jojo's tongue in my mouth makes me want to gag. I turned around to see if anyone was following us. The street's desolate, apart from an old woman rummaging through a garbage can.

We coulda got killed. I felt ill. We stopped at the corner of Avenue C to catch our breath. Two cops cars flew over potholes past us. I felt their speed as they smashed through still air.

They must be going to Tito's. Someone in the building called in the gunshot.

We stood at the light, waiting to cross. Marilyn turned around.

"They didn't stop at the building," she said as we crossed the street.

"What do you mean?" I looked around to see both cop cars turning onto Avenue D.

"No one cares," Marilyn said.

"You think anyone saw us? You think we should go to the cops?" I asked nervously.

Marilyn smiled. "Cops? Hell, no one goes to the cops." I amuse her with my naiveté. She shook her head, laughing at my panic. "We weren't there, we saw nothing . . . Whatever," she grinned.

I felt for the three fat bundles in my bra, and smiled back at her.

Yeah, whatever . . .

Michael Albo

MICHAEL ALBO is a Los Angeles–based author and journalist who has written about crime, music, and popular culture. He is a regular contributor to the *LA Weekly* and the *Los Angeles Times*. His work has also appeared in the *Chicago Tribune*, *Premiere* magazine, *Men's Edge* magazine, and *Sonic Boomers* music magazine. From 1993–2003, he served as the editor of *Hustler Erotic Video Guide*, which he describes as "a half-assed, porn-world version of *People* magazine."

baby, i need to see a man about a duck
by michael albo

Having the habit is an exercise in living undercover, and all afternoon my cover's been blown apart by degrees.

It was coming down evening on a hot and smoggy September day, and I wheeled a dusty white Ford Ranger pickup truck with bald tires and no air-conditioning through moderate traffic on the southbound 605 freeway. The asphalt was tinged blood-red by a sinking sun. This section of freeway carved through a surreal, heat-blasted moonscape of an alluvial fan near the confluence of the nearly dry San Gabriel and Rio Hondo rivers. I was on my way back home from Johnny Gato's ranchita in Irwindale, and I carried just enough drugs to warrant a solid felony charge. The big, white, pissed-off, gimp-legged Long Island duck that I had secured in a cardboard box was escaping its makeshift cell and it was going to be one fucked-up situation if—or, more likely, when—it broke free in the tight confines of that cab. The white head and yellow beak had already crowned. I regretted passing up Johnny Gato's offer to seal the box with duct tape and I regretted even more the decision to let the duck, that I named Quacky, ride up front.

Four hours earlier, I hadn't seen any of this developing. I was a world away in Beverly Hills with a real-life porn slut.

She called herself Eve Eden. "My real name's Eve," she drawled in that insincere way hustlers have when they're laying down the whore con, "and I used to work at this strip club back home called the Garden of Eden, so I use that for my last name." "Back home" was some dismal, bug-infested, malarial Alabama swamp, but Eve had left that all behind to make her sinuous way through the big city as a freshly minted adult-movie starlet. After two weeks in the neon-lit, subterranean depths of Greater Los Angeles, she had come around to realize that she was a lot farther from home than she could ever measure by miles. Attractive enough, but not beautiful, she wore heavy bangs and a pink eye patch to cover the results of girlhood run-in with the business end of a pellet gun. "My brother was huntin' squirrels and he accidentally shot me," she explained. "If I hold a strong magnet to my eye, I can feel the pellet move. It's trippy. It's still in there." She lifted the patch and flashed a milky orb tinted by a smear of blue that was no doubt thankful for all the things it had never seen. She said it was an embarrassment to her. "The kids at school called me Cyclops . . . or Blinky," she said. She wasn't the kind of girl who got many eye-to-eye gazes these days, not since she bought herself a pair of ridiculously enhanced breasts that jutted from her chest like a pair of twin defense missiles and were sheathed in a tight, glittery pink tube top that read, *PORN WHORE.* The pastel pink of her outfit, the patch, the matching pink-frost lipstick and nail polish, and her overly dyed and fried blond hair made her look like a serving of carnival cotton candy that had lost a few bites before being tossed on the midway for the ants that crawled in the dust.

We sat at a table in the sun-splintered dining room of Mary Kate's, a precious and overly fussy Beverly Hills parody of a workingman's chop house on Wilshire Boulevard. She drew the attention from an early lunch crowd of bankers, business squares, and locals with money. It wasn't her clothes or overt whorishness that pulled eyes, but her absolutely white-trash table manners. She was loud, and she was mightily impressed by the complimentary sourdough. "Oh . . . my . . . GOD! This is the best bread I ever ate!"

d in oversized plaid, was a homunculus the
I recognized him right off as a washed-up
h the improbable name of Lemuel Wash-
had once starred in a popular sitcom about
a disadvantaged, pint-sized black child who
der the care of a wealthy, white, industrial-
ons that escaped me, the show had acquired
cult following in the years after its cancella-
ght it was paternalistic and racist, but I never
Maybe I had missed something. I did know that
e catch phrase, which had entered the popular
me like words seldom did. And as I reached the
a gold-toothed grin at me and said it in a thick
ou don' wan' know 'bout dat!" He laughed while

admit it, but he was right. I didn't want to know
no idea who was hustling who at this point, but
re getting awfully friendly with each other. Lemuel
hair but graciously invited me to join them. "Pull up
," he said.

ped, "He's a RAPPER!" I had read somewhere that
o revive his career through thug-rap and it amused
that this young man, who had been a child TV star
that, a pint-sized pitchman for a number of national
TV commercials, could convince anyone that he was
criminal fresh off the streets. But the proof was right in
e. It was obvious Eve thought she had traded up from
here was no sense in sticking around. There would be no
dy floss for dessert.

aned in close to her and said, "Baby, I need to see a man
duck." It was a euphemism I used when going to cop dope
ny Gato's, since he lived on a small ranch overrun by poul-

she crowed. She used a steak knife to slather a crusty piece with an ungodly amount of pale yellow churned cream and suggestively licked the blade clean. She was fascinated by my order of spaghetti all'aglio e olio. "I've never had THAT! Is that what real Eye-talians eat? Can I try some?" I handed her a fork and tablespoon so she could do the proper noodle-twirl like a civilized girl, but she reached past me with a bare hand and grabbed a big, oily handful, leaned her head back, and dropped it down her gullet like a fledgling eating worms. "That IS good!" she smiled through oil-slicked lips. In another setting, it might have been sexy.

The last thing a dope fiend needs or wants is attention. A steady stream of misdirection needs to flow to present yourself as close to normal to the always-watching world around you. I had three simple tricks: I kept a job, I wore a business suit, and I drank. The current job was running a pornographic magazine from an office in an imposing black-glass tower in the heart of Beverly Hills for a limping, moon-faced Greek millionaire. He trundled along with the aid of an ebony cane with a silver and gold lion's head for the handle. The eyes were set with diamonds. He didn't actually need the prop, but told me once that it conferred "power and respect" upon him from underlings like me. I didn't argue. He signed my checks and as long as the copy got in on time and sales didn't fall, I remained an employed and productive member of society. The job also provided an excuse to use the company expense account to entertain feature subjects like Eve, who had just shot a centerfold layout for us. Right now, though, she was turning into a lunchroom liability. Even though I was dressed in my somber navy suit, blue oxford shirt, and mirror-shined black wingtips, the other diners had shifted some of their attention from Eve onto me . . . as if I was supposed to do something about her behavior. And this is why I drank: Americans are a lot more likely to forgive a drunk than they are a dope fiend, and, usually, social mistakes can be glossed over by the simple statement, "I've had a little too much."

Until now, I'd done just fine topping off my daily doses of tar with Wild Turkey 101 served over ice or Bombay Sapphire martinis, both generally backed by freebase cocaine, a stash of which I always kept hidden above a ceiling tile in my office. Today, however, was different. When I ordered a very dry martini and the starch-shirted, whey-faced waiter brought it to our table, I gagged at the poisonous bloom of raw alcohol on my tongue. Eve, her mouth still smeared with butter and oil, and who initially declined my offer of a cocktail, said, "Give me that!" before downing the glass in one gulp. Well, it was supposed to be a thank-you lunch for doing her shoot for far below her day rate . . . as long as she was assured of being the cover girl.

"May I bring something else, sir?" whispered the waiter.

"Uh, yeah. Can you have the bartender make me a double piña colada? But make sure that he puts it in a regular tumbler and leaves off the fruit salad and paper umbrella," I said with a lot of shame. It's not a very masculine drink.

"Absolutely, sir."

"I'll have another martini," chimed Eve, then added with cartoonish lasciviousness, "and make it *diiiirrrty* this time."

She hadn't bothered to wipe her mouth and continued to help herself to my plate of spaghetti with her bare hand and it was driving me to distraction. When the waiter came back with our drinks, I gulped the frothy kiddie-cocktail so fast it gave me a headache. I registered that pineapple and coconut completely masked the taste of the rum. I also noted that my morning dose was wearing off and I'd better do something quick to maintain my equilibrium. I excused myself and made my way into the single-occupancy restroom.

Once the door was securely locked and I was alone in that tomb of green marble, black porcelain, and mirrored walls, I fished

try, a pig or two, and several goats. Most people just took it as a goodbye. I breathed in her whore aroma: too much perfume, gin, stale tobacco, Juicy Fruit gum, and, underneath it all, a musky, feminine funk. It made me even more pissed off at the sawed-off little runt who was twisting a gold pinky ring on his finger. I straightened up and said, "You guys enjoy yourselves. Order what you want! It's all taken care of."

"You all right, homeboy!" said Lemuel.

I nodded and made my way to the front of the restaurant where I tipped the day-shift manager fifty dollars of my own money. I was a good customer and was in there at least twice a week. I always tipped him and the staff well and made sure to introduce him to the girls I brought in. He appreciated it. "Look, man, that guy sitting at my table said he'd pay the tab today, so I'm out of here," I said, pointing at Lemuel.

"I used to watch him on TV when he was a kid," replied the manager, a chubby middle-aged guy in browline specs and a floral-print tie who was not beyond being impressed with whatever celebrities, great or small, entered his domain. "He was funny. What was that thing he used to say?"

"*You don' wan' know 'bout dat!*" I said, certain that Lemuel didn't want to know that he just got stuck with the check.

I didn't see this as shady or underhanded. A good junkie can always justify his actions. This was revenge, and it felt good.

I walked past the valet stand and navigated through several blocks of side streets to get to my truck. Beverly Hills parking could be pricey, but if you knew where to look, and didn't mind a little walk, you could always get a few hours for free. There were never parking concerns at Johnny Gato's, and I set my wheels east and made the afternoon drive in less than an hour, a good time for a Friday.

* * *

Johnny Gato's place wasn't much to look at from the dirt access road that led up to it. A small stucco house, built before World War II, garishly painted raspberry and turquoise with a sagging porch and lots of shade trees, it nested down in a spot between the freeway and the San Gabriel River. In the front yard, two of Johnny's kids, Junior and Angel, had hoisted and secured a bicycle frame from the limb of a live oak tree. They had chopped and lengthened the frame with steel tubing and were preparing to spray-paint it and mint another one of their two-wheeled low-rider creations. It was certain that these two preteen criminals, in their tube-socks, cutoff khakis, and starched white T-shirts with a vertical crease that cut as sharp and vicious as a Saturday-night straight-razor fight, had stolen the frame.

"*Ese*! Your truck looks like shit, eh!" Junior laughed.

"We'll wash it for ten dollars!" said Angel.

"How about I give you guys twenty and you do a good job?"

The boys were fine with that. I crossed the yard and asked, "Just go on in?"

"You always say that, dude. Yes. You don't need to knock. They're in the back," admonished Junior.

I stepped across the rickety flooring of the porch and pushed open a steel-mesh door that squealed out in protest. In the cool darkness of the immaculately kept front room, two old folks, Doña Flor and Don Frank, were watching the Spanish-language news. A woman newscaster was dressed a lot like Eve and was rattling off something in machine-gunfire Spanish.

"Buenas tardes," I offered.

Don Frank pointed at the TV and said, "Can you believe those clothes?"

"It's a crazy world," I replied.

"They're out back," said Doña Flor.

I continued through to the kitchen, which was as surgically

clean as everything else in this tiny house, and saw that Johnny Gato's wife Rose, a big old gal, was working at an ancient stove. A big pot of pinto beans simmered over one burner, and in another, a red stew bubbled. The tight little space smelled of garlic, chilis, and the fresh, citrus tang of cilantro.

"Hey! How you doing?" smiled Rose. "We got birria! One of our goats! You gotta have some."

I had learned a long time ago to never pass up anything Rose offered. Her skill as a housekeeper was surpassed only by her ability as a cook. She moved quickly and filled a bowl with the spicy goat stew, on top of which she stacked some warm corn tortillas and placed a few slices of lime on top of those. I was hungry. I'd only managed a few bites of spaghetti back in Beverly Hills before Eve started slopping her hands into it.

Johnny Gato's head popped in from the door that led to the backyard and field. "Amigo! Bring that stuff with you and eat out here," he invited. He was six feet and 350 pounds of intimidation. His last name wasn't Gato, obviously, but we all called him that because of his resemblance to a fat, mean-eyed cat. Like his kids, he wore the cholo uniform of cutoff khakis, sneakers, and starched T-shirt. His arms were covered with tattoos, acquired in various correctional facilities, that depicted variations of La Adelita, the sombrero-wearing, pistol-packing female warrior icon of the Mexican Revolution. It was a look that worked for him.

"Did you give him any of the peppers?" he asked his wife, who shot him a concerned look.

"No, no," he said, "I've seen this loco eat. He's more hardcore than the kids." Rose plopped a few small green chilis into the stew and I followed Johnny out back.

Underneath the spreading branches of a gnarled and ancient plum tree that was giving up the last of its summer bounty sat a shiftless crew playing dominoes in the late-afternoon sun. By complicated bloodlines and affiliations, we had all known each other since junior high school here in the San Gabriel Valley. Shuffling the tiles was Backyard Bob, who ran a pot-selling enterprise out of his mom's backyard and who rarely left home. Waiting for their bones were the Sorendahl brothers—Tumblin' Dan and Little Gigantor. They were sturdy brawlers and good guys to have on your side if trouble broke out, even if they were usually the cause of it. Tumblin' Dan had been laying low lately. He had earned his nickname from a series of run-ins with the law, each more serious than the last. His downward plunge had been put on hold by a recent embrace of the New Testament, but the boredom of not running wild weighed heavily on him. We all expected a spectacular fuck-up from him any day now.

His younger brother, Little Gigantor, was short, squat, and as powerfully constructed as the space-age Japanese cartoon robot that inspired his name. He was capable of amazing feats of strength and sudden violence. I had been with him on a liquor run one night when we bumped into a spindly little cholo we knew from high school named Manny Saldana. Manny was dusted and wearing a bandanna so low on his brow he needed to tilt his head back to see. He noticed us and wanted a cigarette. "Got a frajo, *ese*?" he asked, and shifted his melon back even further. Quick as a rattlesnake strike, Little Gigantor grabbed him by the collar and belt, spun like an Olympic hammer-thrower, and tossed Manny right through the plate glass window of the liquor store.

"What the fuck did you do that for?" I shouted.

"Did you see the way that punk was looking at me? Nobody challenges me."

"Dude, he didn't challenge you. He was just trying to see from under that stupid rag of his. We need to get the fuck out of here!"

"Aw, don't be such a pussy, doper. I'm getting a twelve-pack first," he said, and calmly walked into the store, bought his beer, and threatened the owner not to call the cops. It must have worked because we made it back without seeing any flashing red and blue lights.

"None of you boys eating?" I asked as I sat down at the redwood picnic table that served as headquarters for this crew.

"We were until Johnny made us try those goddamn chilis," said Tumblin' Dan.

"You guys are a bunch of jotos," assessed Johnny.

I wrapped some birria in a tortilla and dunked it into the red broth. That first bite allowed some grease to coat my tongue—my theory was that it would provide a cushion for the chili. Then I grabbed one slender green stem from the stew, shook it dry, and bit in. Nothing.

"See? That's how you eat a chili!" said Johnny, who slapped me on the back. But as he did, I could feel a warmth build quickly to a fire. I took another bite of birria. That's the trick. A little bit of grease will cut through and dissipate the effects of even the hottest chili. Of course, you still have to deal with the intestinal aftermath, but you'll be able to amaze and impress your friends.

Little Gigantor passed me a sweating bottle of Lucky lager from a cooler while Backyard Bob finished spit-sealing a huge, guppy-shaped hand-rolled joint spiced with freebase cocaine. "Coca-puffs," he cautioned as he took the first hit and passed it on. I declined because I'd be driving home with contraband. Why open the door for a screw-up? I'd never seen the inside of a jail cell and I didn't want to start now.

Johnny Gato sat down next to me and asked, "So, what do you need?"

I pushed away the bowl of birria and told him, "Two grams of the tar and an eight ball of base."

"Two-fifty," he said. Same price as always. "Jorge will take care of it. He's back with the goats. Just go tell him."

This always made me uncomfortable. Jorge was the youngest of Johnny's kids. A fifth-grader. And unlike his two wayward brothers, he was a kid who had a love for reading, science, and school. Of the three boys, I was laying odds on Jorge to be the one who lived long enough to see his twenty-first birthday.

I shuffled across the dust and patchy crabgrass of the backyard and through a chain-link fence that opened onto about two acres of dirt and gravel divided by pens made of galvanized pipe. A couple of hogs wallowed in mud inside one of them. In the other, several small goats were mobbing a little black-haired kid in overalls who scattered feed on the ground.

"Hey, Jorge!" I called.

He knew why I was there. "What do you need?"

"Two and a ball," I told him.

"Just a minute," he said, and heaved the sack of feed outside the pen where it landed near my feet. The goats followed it and stared expectantly at me with their rectangular, demonic pupils.

"Can I feed 'em?" I called after him.

"Go ahead," he said.

I took a handful of pelleted feed from the sack and held it through the rails of the pen as the goats jostled for their share. Jorge had gone off to a rusty steel shed and was in there for about five minutes. When he came out, he was followed by a small flock of quacking white ducks. He handed me a neatly wrapped package. I looked inside; the goods were there. I didn't check closely. I had done business with this family for so long, there was no need. It was always a square deal. The ducks flowed around his feet and concentrated on bullying one of their own that had a malformed foot. It was twisted inward, but its owner didn't seem to be in any pain.

"What's with these ducks?" I asked.

"They don't like that one because he's different with the bad foot," was Jorge's explanation.

"So what do you do?" I wanted to know.

"We'll cook him, probably," was his deadpan reply. "You ever had duck?"

"Yeah. Not a big fan."

"Hey, you got a garden, right?"

"I do. A small one," I answered.

"Why don't you take him home with you? They make good pets . . . and they eat snails," he tossed in, trying to sweeten the deal.

Normally, I wouldn't have acted so impulsively, but Jorge was a good kid and I felt guilty about my part in exposing him to the darker side of adult behavior, so I said, "Tell your dad to get me a box."

Jorge grabbed the duck which sat calmly in his arms as he stroked him, and we walked back to the yard. "He says he'll take the duck, but he needs a box."

First things first, I handed over the cash to Johnny Gato, who pocketed it and went around the side of the house and came back with a cardboard box. He was poking holes in the side with a folding Buck knife.

"How far you going with him?" Johnny asked.

"To Marina del Rey."

"This should be okay then. But maybe we'd better tape the box."

"Nah, we can just weave the flaps. He won't be able to get out."

"Dude, they're pretty strong," cautioned Johnny Gato. But as we put the duck into the box, it settled right in and grew still. "Maybe you're right," he said, sounding awfully unsure.

But now that I had my dope and felt it weighing down my pocket like a two-ton anchor, I wanted to get home, get high, and put the week behind me. I was antsy and needed to go.

"All right, man, I'm gone. Tell Rose thanks for the birria. You boys stay out of trouble," I said. Everybody was used to my quick exits after I copped and they barely looked up from their game of dominoes.

"Just go through the side yard," said Johnny, and slapped my back again.

I walked around the house and into the front yard. I could see that Junior and Angel hadn't washed the truck. "Dude, you didn't give us enough time to even get started!" cried Angel.

"Don't worry. You still get paid . . . but next time I'm here, you give me a wash, right?" I said, and handed them each ten dollars.

"What's in the box?" Junior asked.

"One of Jorge's ducks."

"Good luck with that," said Angel, and made a mock Catholic blessing.

Smart-ass kids, but they were entertaining.

I should have shoved the duck into the bed of the truck, but I didn't want any accidental escapes, so I placed it on the bench seat instead. I walked around to the driver's side, got in, and drove in the direction of the freeway.

Everything was cool until I popped in a Captain Beyond cassette tape as I hit the 605 on-ramp. The duck didn't dig the noise and got agitated. Even after I turned off the music, it only got wilder.

"Shut up, Quacky!" I said as I knocked on the side of his cardboard prison with my fist. That was a mistake that only made the duck more determined to get out.

Once its beak pushed through the cardboard, followed by its head, the duck saw its new surroundings and didn't like them. A tremendous ruckus kicked up as it started flapping its wings, kicking its feet, and pitching a fit. This was a dangerous situation. I kept looking in the rearview mirror to make sure I hadn't picked up the Highway Patrol.

There was no shoulder on the 605 on which to pull off. I took the transition to the eastbound 60 toward Los Angeles as the duck managed to get one twitching wing out of the box. I knew there was a shoulder dead ahead so I eased over and stopped. The duck did not, and kept up its fury of hisses, quacks, and near convulsive efforts to escape. I set the emergency blinkers, got out, and walked around to the passenger side. As I opened the door, Quacky finally burst from the box and shot toward the first avenue of escape it saw. All I could do was get out of the way. *Well, fuck him,* I thought. He could take his gimpy webbed foot and the rest of himself down to the San Gabriel River that lay right below us.

I tried for a minute to shoo the duck over the bridge and into the river, but realized I presented a target of suspicious activity to anyone passing by. Best to let nature sort it out. I got back in the truck and merged into traffic. I looked in the side mirror and saw Quacky take a short and panicked flight right into the front grille of a Mack MH Ultra-Liner. There he stayed, pinned to the chrome like a figurehead on an old-time seagoing freighter. As the rig passed, I gave a solemn wave to poor Quacky. I muttered a quick prayer of thanks that no cops had seen me and continued my drive back home to hearth and high.

There wasn't anything else I could do . . . except to make sure to always tell young Jorge that his duck was doing just fine, strutting in the garden, eating snails, and living the waterfowl high-life.

It made the kid happy.

T. Bogosian

ERIC BOGOSIAN wrote the plays and films *subUrbia* and *Talk Radio* (in which he also starred). He often acts on stage and screen, last appearing on Broadway in Donald Margulies's *Time Stands Still*. His most recent novel is *Perforated Heart*.

godhead
by eric bogosian

A strip of white light falls across a man seated in pitch-black, holding a microphone. He speaks in a slow, deliberate voice with a New Orleans accent.

The way I see it, it's a fucked-up world, it's not going anyplace, nothing good is happening to nobody, you think about it these days and nothing good is happening to anybody and if something good is happening to anybody, it's not happening to me, it's not happening to myself.

The way I see it, there be this man, some man sitting in a chair behind a desk in a room somewhere down in Washington, D.C. See, and this man, he be sitting there, he be thinking about what we should do about crime rate, air pollution, space race . . . Whatever this guy supposed to be thinking about. And this guy, he be sitting down there and thinking, and he be thinking about what's happenin' in *my* life . . . he be deciding on food stamps, and work programs, and the welfare, and the medical aid and the hospitals, whether I be working today. Makin' all kinds a decisions for me. He be worrying about how I spen' my time! Then he lean back in his ol' leather chair, he start thinkin' about da nukular bomb. He be deciding whether I live or die today! Nobody makes those decisions for me. That's for me to decide. I decide when I want to get up in da mornin', when I want to work, when I want to play, when I want to do shit! That's my decision. I'm free. When I die, that's up to God or somebody, not some guy sittin' in a chair. See?

I just wanna live my life. I don't hurt nobody. I turn on the TV set, I see the way everybody be livin'. With their swimming pools and their cars and houses and living room with the fireplace in the living room . . . There's a fire burnin' in the fireplace, a rug in front of the fireplace. Lady. She be lyin' on the rug, evenin' gown on . . . jewelry, sippin' a glass o' cognac . . . She be lookin' in the fire, watchin' the branches burnin' up . . . thinkin' about things. Thinkin'. Thinkin'. What's she thinkin' about?

I jus' wanna live my life. I don't ask for too much. I got my room . . . got my bed . . . my chair, my TV set . . . my needle, my spoon, I'm okay, see? I'm okay.

I get up in the mornin', I combs my hair, I wash my face. I go out. I hustle me up a couple a bags a D . . . new works if I can find it.

I take it back to my room, I take that hairwon. I cook it up good in the spoon there . . . I fill my needle up.

Then I tie my arm [*caressing his arm*] . . . I use a necktie, it's a pretty necktie, my daughter gave it to me . . . Tie it tight . . . pump my arm . . . then I take the needle, I stick it up into my arm . . . find the hit . . . blood . . .

Then I undoes the tie . . . I push down on that needle [*pause*] . . . and I got everything any man ever had in the history of this world. Jus' sittin' in my chair . . .

[*Voice lower*] I got love and I got blood. That's all you need. I can feel that blood all going up behind my knees, into my stomach, in my mouth I can taste it . . . Sometimes it goes back down my arm, come out the hole . . . stain my shirt . . .

I know . . . I know there's people who can't handle it. Maybe I can't handle it. Maybe I'm gonna get all strung out and fucked up . . .

. . . Even if I get all strung out and fucked up, don't make no difference to me . . . Even I get that hepatitis and the broken veins and the ulcers on my arms . . . addicted. Don't make no difference to me. I was all strung out and fucked up in the first place . . .

Life is a monkey on my back. You ride aroun' in your car, swim in your warm swimming pool. Watch the fire . . . I don't mind. I don't mind at all. Just let me have my taste. Have my peace. Jus' leave me be. Jus' leave me be.

[*Turns in toward the dark*]

Jervey Tervalon

JERVEY TERVALON is the author of several books, including the novels *Serving Monster* and *Dead Above Ground*, and coeditor, with Gary Phillips, of *The Cocaine Chronicles*. He is currently directing the Literature for Life project. Literature for Life is a new kind of forum: part literary magazine, part educational resource center, part salon. Writers, journalists, artists, and educators come together to ignite young minds while celebrating the diversity of Los Angeles.

gift horse
by jervey tervalon

eroin didn't blow up in the neighborhood, not like red devils and weed. We held out for rock cocaine to go insane and then we burned shit up until there was nothing left to burn. But heroin did make a run at us—one fine spring the white devil drug appeared with the help of a banged-up Nova turning the corner, tires squealing as it fishtailed along Second Avenue and the fool at the wheel with the big afro flung a brown bag out the window, and then a roller took the turn *French Connection*–style, and should have caught that knucklehead in the Nova before the next corner, but he drove like a nigga who had nothing to lose but doing life.

I sat on the porch with Sidney sitting across from me with his nice-ass leather jacket on, sipping a Mickey's Big Mouth; ignoring my comic book–reading pootbutt ass like I was invisible. I knew he was waiting on my brother to make a run for weed or red devils or whatever. I wasn't surprised that he didn't have a spare word for me, and I didn't mind because I hated motherfucking Sidney. He wasn't obvious about being a dick to me except for the time he broke my finger because I made the mistake of trying to save a seat on the couch. Should have figured that he'd ignore my hand and flop down, and yeah, he broke my little finger and I knew he didn't care even with all those fake apologies to my mama. Sidney and my brother just kept watching the Rams while I had to go to the hospital to get a splint. He was my nemesis, though it wasn't much of a contest with me being fifteen. I couldn't hang with just throwing a punch at his smug face. Jude, my brother, didn't have a high opinion of me, saying I started shit and pissed people off so I shouldn't be expecting him to have my back.

The roar of the big engine of the roller drifted away and my attention turned to the brown bag at the curb. Sidney gave me a sinister grin and sauntered over to it, hiked his pressed jeans a bit, glanced about as though he was daring the police to roll up on him, and nonchalantly picked it up and returned to the porch. He examined the contents of the paper bag; about a hundred little baggies with powder inside.

"What's that?" I asked.

"What's what?"

"What's inside the baggies?"

"Nothing," he said, and walked away like he was on top of the world, and Sydney always looked like he was on top of the world.

Though I hated him, I couldn't help admiring his style. He didn't fight, or carry a gun, he never engaged in open hostility. He won a lofty position in the neighborhood because of his ability to get along with anybody who was worth anything to get along with, and his ability to make everybody trust him completely, except for me, and I didn't count. Once they trusted him, Sydney would get in on what was good, and leave the rest. He had a great talent that made everything work; he talked better than anybody and he knew everything. He knew how to sell drugs in such a way that he never seemed to be dealing, and thus, he had an understated pimp-splendor thing happening. He rode a tricked-out metallic blue chopper with an airbrushed image of a flying saucer hovering over Los Angeles on the gas tank; and this was before his heroin windfall.

Sidney's dealings were all undercover except for Leslie, the sheboonie up the street who wore curlers, slippers, and a matching bathrobe. Youngsters thought she was an ugly-ass woman until you saw her up close and you realized she was a dude who wanted to be an ugly-ass woman. He would show up at Sidney's door, which Sidney told him not to do—who really wanted a sheboonie coming to the house?—early in the morning to get some stepped-on baggies of powder, because even though I didn't know a thing about heroin, I knew that Sidney would toss in all kinds of shit to stretch it and keep that money flowing. Leslie shared her heroin with Norman Zerka, the dude who was so light-skinned that even with his lame afro, no one was sure if he was black or not. Norman took to living with Leslie because he liked that heroin high and he even left Bernadette, the woman who was supposed to be his wife, cause she couldn't afford to keep him stoned like he wanted to be. I didn't mind Norman cause he was polite, and didn't break my fingers. He always had hot shit to sell, nice bikes he would jack at UCLA from the white boys, but people who knew better wouldn't buy his magic television, like my mother did. "I can't pass up this great deal," she said, and Norman, polite as always, brought back her change for a ten, and sold her this really new-looking, all-white and shiny, tiny television that my mama placed in the kitchen so we could eat dinner and watch Alfred Hitchcock movies. But Norman wasn't really selling the hot television, he was renting it. Within a week, he sneaked in the house and stole the television back and sold it to somebody else.

Sidney, who had already been the king of the neighborhood, and now seemed to be king of the world, lived exactly like he had lived before, but with more aplomb. One sunny afternoon, he was holding court under the big pine tree. He sat there on the fire hydrant, a six-pack near his feet, with most of the fellas in the neighborhood laughing at his jokes and drinking his Heinekens.

"I don't know about you knuckleheads, but I'm going on vacation."

"Where to?" Henry-Hank, the neighborhood's handsome idiot asked.

"Amsterdam."

Everyone nodded as though they knew where and what he was talking about.

"You can smoke weed in coffee houses. Police don't fuck with you and the women are cool and don't mind taking care of you."

Who could argue with Sidney's success? He had a plan, and the funds to pull it off. I imagined myself kicking it with beautiful blond women; then I shook that nonsense out of my head. That was a mistake; suddenly they noticed me, particularly my brother. Usually, he was too high to care.

"What you doing here! Take your ass home. Hang out with Googie, somebody your own age," he said.

I shrugged and walked away, making a slow meandering circle and ending up exactly where I had been in the first place. Then, as if by instinct, the fellas uprooted themselves and ended up at my house. As long as my mother was at work, the fellas—an ever-changing number of brothers who would hold sway on the lawn or in the living room, smoking weed and watching sports, or drinking beer on the beautiful Saint Augustine grass that my dad had planted before he and my mother divorced—kicked it at our house. I listened to them argue about the Lakers and the Rams, and I even heard an argument about whether or not H.P. Lovecraft was racist. Then Henry-Hank appeared, agitated as Lassie with an urgent message.

"Sidney is passed out, facedown in the ivy in front of his house."

Weed and beer might make you mellow, but everybody was now alert and hustling to Sidney's house.

Henry-Hank was right; there was Sidney, facedown in the ivy, looking stylishly dead.

Jude squatted next to him and shook his shoulder.

"He ain't dead, he's passed out."

Jude and Lil' Dell lifted him up and walked him up the steps and knocked on the door.

Mrs. Green opened the door and for a moment was shocked, but then she looked so angry that it didn't seem she cared that her son was right there, drooling, head lolling about.

"What did you do to my boy? Did y'all get him drunk?"

Jude, never too quick on the uptake, just shook his head. "I didn't get him drunk."

"Well, he's drunk; he's even pissed on himself."

"Like I said, we didn't get him drunk."

She opened the door and Jude and Lil' Dell dragged him to the couch and tossed him on it.

Sidney wasn't much good for anything after that. Every day he was fucked up, passed out on somebody's lawn or porch, or maybe unconscious in the backseat of somebody's car. I got to wondering about heroin then, how somebody as social as Sidney would decide to leave what he was behind, and become something else altogether: a straight dope fiend. He stopped selling weed and red devils and he certainly wasn't going to be selling his stash of heroin; he was running through it like Halloween candy.

Mrs. Green came home from work one day to see all the furniture turned upside down and ripped apart; nothing was stolen as far as she knew other than the cute little television Sidney had picked up for her from Norman Zerka. But Sidney knew what had been stolen—the basis for his economic existence and his happiness—and he was right out on the street looking for it.

Sidney, possessed of super ghetto cool, walked around the neighborhood in such casual good humor that if you didn't know him you'd think he was on top of the world. And despite Sidney having been robbed of his livelihood, his mother kept him in spending money, a whole lot of spending money, because she made serious cash running the Department of Recreation and Parks for the city of Los Angeles. Sidney began buying beer for anyone who wandered onto the corner under the big tree. He let Henry-Hank have a Heineken, even Googie. I could have had one myself, but I didn't like the taste of beer and didn't want to be beholden to Sidney. All the generosity was not how I knew Sidney to be. It didn't take a genius to figure out why; he needed information.

It almost looked normal around the neighborhood with Sidney back on his throne passing the joint around like how it used to be done before the heroin descended upon Second Avenue. He just took it when the running joke got to be asking him if he had any red devils, and he'd just shrug, smile broadly, open his arms, and say, "Wish I did," or, "Red devils, me?"

A week or so later, Sidney getting ripped off was history, and he was ready to make his move. Googie told me Sidney had showed up at his window, rapping on it just loud enough not to wake his daddy. In a few minutes Googie stumbled outside buckling up his overalls.

"What it be like?" Googie asked, trying to sound hard and hiding how excited he was to have Sidney, even in his fallen state, blessing his house with his presence. Sidney sat on a wooden picnic table, near the patio, smoking a square. He offered Googie one, and Googie wanted it, knowing that he couldn't handle it, even a menthol. He reached for it and Sidney yanked it away and laughed.

"Does your daddy let you smoke now?"

"I don't know. Maybe I should ask your mama," Googie said, and headed back into the house.

"Hey, Googie, don't go away mad. I got a money-making proposition that I know you're going to like."

"What's that?"

"I want you to hang out at Leslie's house. She likes to play *Monopoly* and shit. Get into one of them games. Keep your eyes open to where Norman Zerka might have the stash. I'm sure that's the fool who ripped me off."

Whatever Googie felt before, the giddiness of making money, the pride at having Sidney cajoling him to do a favor—all of that vanished. In its place was a Fatburger, pink at the center with a runny egg on top, queasiness.

"You want me to kick it with a sheboonie?"

Sidney shrugged. "I ain't asking you to be one."

"If you think they got it, why don't you just strong arm them and get it back?"

Sidney drew on his cigarette. "Norman Zerka, no problem. Leslie might be a sheboonie, but she can straight beat the shit out of you and she's strapped and knows how to shoot. Once, Lil' Dil tried to steal her purse, and she said, *You made me jump out of my femaleness, back into my maleness, and now I'm gonna kick your ass!* And she did, beat his ass south and north. She was a paratrooper when she was living as a man. She went through jump school with Jimi Hendrix."

"Jimi who?" Googie didn't hear any of that; what he heard was what Sidney wanted him to do. It wasn't something he wanted to do—chance getting beat down by a sheboonie for the world to know. *Fuck that!* "I ain't cool with this. Get somebody else to do it," Googie said, and turned around again.

"I'll give you forty dollars."

Googie pivoted like Kareem doing an up-and-under. "Fifty, up front."

"Aw, I see you learning how to negotiate," Sidney said, and pulled two twenties and a ten off a roll and flicked them to Googie; floating weirdly, they reached his hand.

"You help me get my shit back and I'll give you twice that much."

"What? A hundred fifty?"

Sidney squinted. "Don't they teach you anything at school? You knuckleheads can't multiply."

"Shit, I can multiply. Ask me eight times eight! It's sixty-four! How about six times six? It's thirty-six!"

"What's nine times eight?" Sidney asked.

"Ninety-eight," Googie responded, with the confidence of a pathologically bad guesser.

Sidney shook his head. "Yep, your ass really knocked that out of the park."

Googie wanted to say *Fuck you*, but he felt the crisp bills in hand and instead watched Sidney walk away into the darkness of the alley.

"Naw, man, I'm not cool with that," I said.

"I'll give you five dollars."

"Your ass just said Sidney gave you fifty. I'm gonna be hanging with you at the sheboonie's house and I'm getting one-tenth of what you got for doing the same thing!"

I sipped my Strawberry Crush shaking my head, waiting for Googie to come back at me. I knew something was up since he'd knocked on my door with a drink and chili Fritos for me. I knew I should have asked why he was bringing me something, cause usually his ass would be trying to bum a quarter off of me. I sat on the porch while he stretched out on the lawn like the fellas did, looking as rakish as a fat boy can look.

"I ain't kicking it with a sheboonie. Nope. I ain't rolling with you so you can find Sidney's lost heroin. I'm going to college. I ain't doing knucklehead shit like that."

Googie snorted. "Look, if you never do anything, how's that

living? You always talking about tomorrow—what if you get hit by a car and die? Then all the shit you could have been doing, you didn't do, and what did that get you? You just missed out."

"You saying I need to kick it with a sheboonie before I die? That don't make no kind of sense."

Googie's face trembled and he looked genuinely hurt, like a huge baby about ready to cry. I knew he was going to come back pleading something ridiculous. "Aw . . . come on . . . I thought we were ace-boon-coon pardners. We go way back, don't leave me hanging, I wouldn't do that—shit, you remember when I saved your ass at that dance at Forshay?"

He finished but I knew that it wouldn't stop, that he would keep at me until I either slapped him or gave in.

"If we going to go, let's roll. I ain't going over there at night. Don't know what kind of shit goes down over there at night."

We walked the two blocks in silence. I hung back when he got to the door, hoping that no one would notice me. After he knocked, it seemed like nobody was home, which was cool. Then the door swung open so abruptly that Googie covered his head and ran. There was Leslie in an aquamarine bathrobe with matching curlers and fuzzy slippers, wearing lots of makeup on her strangely girlish face.

"Hey, Leslie."

"What are you doing here?" she asked in a voice that sounded sort of womanly and sort of mannish, but weirder than usual because she was slurring her words.

"You want to play *Monopoly*? I heard you're good. Me and Garvy like to play."

It seemed like it took a second for the words to register in Leslie's buzzing brain, but she nodded.

"Yeah, I love me some *Monopoly*, but Norman is always too fucked up for board games," Leslie said, and waved for Googie to follow. Her robe opened revealing smooth, brown, muscular legs that sent Googie into a panic. He looked about for me but I waved to him from the sidewalk.

"Where's your friend going?"

"I think his mama called him. He's chicken-shit like that," Googie said, and before I could run he was already on me, and grabbed my arm in a sweaty, iron grip and dragged me through the open door into Leslie's house. We smelled sweet, cloying incense and strange music playing, singing and shit, and trumpets.

"You don't like Billie Holiday?" Leslie asked.

"Who's he?" Googie replied.

"Sit down," Leslie said, ignoring the question, and handed Googie the game. "Do you want something to drink?"

"You got a joint?" Googie asked.

Leslie laughed. "We do not do drugs in my house." She laughed again and coughed. "You set up the board and I'll get us something to drink."

Soon as she left the room, Googie stood. "You set up the game, I'm gonna check shit out."

Googie casually searched the immaculate house—all the furniture covered in plastic with plastic runners protecting the carpets—as though the heroin would spring up and land in his hand.

"You wasting your time. Let's bail," I said, but Googie just got on his knees to look under the couch.

Leslie returned with 7UPs on a lacquered tray.

"I hope you boys are good. I hate to waste my time with rookies."

Googie snorted, "I kick much butt at *Monopoly*."

They began to play and we both saw just how sprung Leslie was for the game. She rolled dice and skipped her silver dog about the board, laughing too hard, even drooling a little. Googie glanced at me a few times and I shook my head. I had no idea of how this was going to go; how this was going to work out in his favor. All I wanted was to get the fuck out of there, especially after Leslie started getting all flirty and taking turns tickling us. Homechick wasn't going away and all she wanted to do was kick our asses at *Monopoly*, and she was. Well anyway, Googie was up fifty dollars on Sidney and that wasn't bad, but I wasn't up on Sidney, not a dime.

"I'm going to use the bathroom for a bit," she said after a while, looking kind of irritated.

"Let's bail," I said to Googie, but he shook me off and started searching again. I tried the front door but it was deadlocked. Googie returned to the table trying to figure out a plan, but soon we both noticed Leslie hadn't returned.

Finally, we got tired of waiting and found her passed out on the floor of the bathroom, needle in arm, like Sidney when he had that shit. With her robe twisted around her waist, we saw her weird-looking leather panties with rhinestones.

"Yeah, you know, freaks got to be freaky." Googie shrugged and went about the house looking for the heroin, and wondering where Norman Zerka might be. I hung by the door, but Googie called to me. He found Norman in the master bedroom, passed out across the narrow bed, with his head hanging on one side and his feet the other, pale like the sun never shined on his white ass, even if he had a big fucking 'fro, and just about naked except he wore the same leather panties as Leslie, like that bald chick with the whip on the Ohio Players cover. Googie looked over the room but didn't find anything except for empty baggies with white residue sticking to them. Sidney was shit out of luck.

"These muthafucking weirdos ran through the heroin faster than Sidney thought they would. Dope fiends," Googie said, as we shoved each other trying to climb through the bedroom window first. I won, but then Googie noticed the little white television near Norman Zerka's head. He snagged it and finished climbing through the window.

"Hey, man, that's my mama's television."

"Yeah, how it get in there?" he asked, and handed it to me.

"Norman stole it from her after selling it."

"Yeah, well, now we stole it back."

We walked home, Googie talking about what he'd tell Sidney; maybe that the dope was still there and exactly where to find it for another twenty . . . fuck that, another fifty. A nigga needed to get paid these days; times were tough in 1972.

"Yeah, but I didn't get shit except the chili Fritos you brought me."

"What's that in your hands? You got your mama's little television back. It all worked out."

Or so it seemed. A few days later, a VW Bug driven by Norman Zerka stopped in front of Googie's house as he was watering the lawn, and Leslie sprang out still in curlers, bathrobe, and slippers, and caught Googie with an overhand right and dropped him flat on his back with the hose shooting wild around him. He came over and told me this, with his eye swollen and purple, looking around like he might get clocked again.

Me, I stayed inside and watched that little white television until I heard that Leslie and Norman had left town after robbing the Security Pacific Bank on Jefferson. On the corner, I heard Sidney, who had found himself another stash of red devils and was back to dealing—though the heroin was gone for good—say that they were living like Bonnie and Clyde, robbing banks up and down the coast.

"Romantic motherfuckers," he said, while lighting another joint.

PART III

GETTING A GRIP

LYDIA LUNCH is always rebelling against the hypocrisy of America's picture-perfect Hollywood image, which it exports through television, films, and commercial music. Her art has always revealed the down-and-dirty side of the all-too-real American underbelly. She is the author of *Paradoxia* and *Will Work for Drugs*, both published by Akashic Books.

ghost town
by lydia lunch

Never answer the door at five forty-five a.m. on a Sunday morning. Either somebody's too high, somebody has just died, or somebody has just arrived who wants to kill you.

I drove 2,777 miles just to get away from him. From the Hudson River to the Pacific Ocean and it still wasn't far enough away.

A low-brow dirt bike racer from Topanga Canyon who was hell bent on a cross-country creepy crawl had pulled up, swept me off my feet, threw me into the front seat of his dilapidated pickup truck, and headed west, gunning it at full speed until we hit the "Slum by the Sea": Venice, California. He said he was on a rescue mission to save me. That he had been sent east by a mutual friend who was concerned for my safety after hearing stories about hospital stays and late-night 911 calls. Great, the sociopath abducts the schizophrenic out from under the psychopath in a late-night snatch-and-grab.

Something had to give because I was at the breaking point. The burned-out buildings, uncollected garbage, broken streetlights, endless break-ins, chronic shake-downs, and general havoc wreaked on the streets of New York City's Lower East Side, circa 1979, were a cake walk next to the damage being done in my own apartment. The alcoholic pill-popping Irish construction worker who I'd been holed up with for the past few months was getting mean.

Jealous, cruel, and beautiful. An irresistible combination of mania and machismo. By day he'd play iron man. Up at the crack of six sporting boxers and a wife beater, Lucky Strike behind his left ear, throwing sandwiches in a bag, filling a thermos with black coffee and Irish whiskey, singing a silly rockabilly song, a sly smile dancing under sleepy green eyes, happy to just be alive as he kissed me goodbye and disappeared out the door. Everything hunky dory until the sun went down, the knives came out, and he stumbled back from the bar half plastered after banging steel girders together for another eight-hour stretch. The first thirty minutes were always filled with bliss. We'd kiss, fall back onto the bed, and batter our bodies into each other until one of us started bleeding. Then batter away a little more after swallowing a couple of Seconals with a back of Johnnie Walker Black.

And that, my friend, is where the trouble came in. Loverboy loved his booze more than he loved me, and in return the booze hated my fucking guts. Probably because I refused to play slave to it and only used it as a lubricant for pharmaceuticals. A treacherous combination which triggered the bitch that provoked the bastard and resulted in a fucking that felt more like fighting, and the fighting would flare up over some petty jealous bullshit usually concerning who I was or wasn't fucking while the dick was dry humping rebar over at the construction site breaking his goddamn ass, and on and on until the garbage trucks rumbled on their early-morning run and he'd pass out for two or three hours, waking up refreshed and ready to greet the day as if nothing had happened, with a "Good mornin', darlin', care for a cup of joe?" as he smiled whistling through his wolfen teeth.

If Brando did *Badlands* while stoned on barbiturates and booze . . . well . . . you get the picture. The one that played in rerun like a bad Turner Classic that our TV eyes got stuck on night after night for weeks on end.

Yeah . . . yeah, and so it went, so wrapped up in torturing the shit out of each other that the world outside our ghetto hidey-hole was a squirrel-gray cotton-candy haze that we were too fucked up to realize didn't muffle the screeching or screams forever leaching out the windows and reverberating into the street below, and if anyone was tuned in they probably could have heard us all the way to the West Coast. Our psychosis getting carried away like radio frequencies emitting toxic shock waves into the ionosphere. I needed to get the fuck out. And fast.

I spiked his drink, packed a bag, left a note, and climbed into the front seat of the grease monkey's pickup truck, which was parked on the corner of 12th Street and Avenue B where he had been waiting for me to show up for thirty-six hours so that he could "save me."

Four days later we landed in Ghost Town. A grungy biker and his nubile Las Vegas bride, a bitchy witch dressed in black casting voodoo glances at the neighboring hood rats. They probably feared the look on my face more than I feared what they hid in their waistbands. The gangbangers left me alone. But the ghosts wouldn't. They were everywhere.

Some people are afraid of ghosts and what lurks in the dark. Terrified of the possibility of the unseen violators sneaking around within its murky shadows. But true evil is arrogant by nature and doesn't always bother to hide its intentions under the cloak of night. It gathers even more power by flaunting its vigor in the unadulterated glare of a perpetual high noon.

Los Angeles. A beautifully hideous sprawl. Stretching like an ever-expanding virus of sick contagion under the relentless sun as hot Devil Winds blow down from the mountains scorching the landscape. The promise of an endless summer shattered by gunshots and sirens, helicopters and hospital beds.

In 1980, Los Angeles County reported 51,448 violent crimes, 27,987 cases of aggravated assault, and 1,011 murders. The Sunset Strip Slayers preyed on young women, ex-lovers, and each other's twisted fantasies as they played out depraved rituals with the de-capitated head of one of their victims. Welcome to Hollywood, asshole, where anything is possible.

New York City may have been bankrupt, decrepit, and suffer-ing from the final stages of rigor mortis, but the California Dream was a waking nightmare of dead-end streets ripe with bloated corpses where bad beat poets, dope-sick singers, cracked actors, and petty criminals were all praying to a burned-out star on the sidewalk. All betting on a chance encounter which would flip the script in the lousy late-night made-for-TV movie of their wasted lives. I guess I was no different.

Everything was fucking peaches and whipped cream for the first six months of matrimonial bliss, until the lunatic who rescued me from the maniac took a bad spill on the Pacific Coast Highway and ended up in a coma with two charges of vehicular manslaugh-ter on his rap sheet and a letter at the side of his bed which threat-ened eviction from our Venice crash pad. I went home and started to pack my bags.

In the same way that a shark can smell blood, a junkie's sixth sense alerts him to any possible random opportunity that may arise in which he can hustle, steal, score, or move in on and take advan-tage of an unsuspecting mark's benevolent disposition, a friend's temporary weakness, or an ex-girlfriend's first night alone in a near-empty house. It was five forty-five a.m. on a Sunday morn-ing when the doorbell blasted and shattered what was left of my nerves.

Impeccable timing. The bastard always had it. Even down to the way he smoked a cigarette as I opened the door. Holding it down between thumb and index, deep drag, a small puckering sound as he pulled it away from his lips, staring straight into my eyes before he flung the butt into the wet grass. A sadistic smirk creeping in and cracking up the left side of his face. His husky whisper, hypnotic and irresistible . . . "Good mornin', darlin', spare a cup of joe for the road warrior?"

The Irish construction worker. One hundred and ninety-three days later and a distance of almost three thousand miles meant nothing to the madman convinced he could walk right in whistling Dixie and simply steal me back. Don't laugh. I let him in.

With the cunning of a snake that can sense whether or not you're about to attack it first, a schizophrenic can detect the atmospheric flux in a psychopath's gravitational force field. Something inside him had shifted slightly since I last saw him. His magnetism seemed less manic. More mesmerizing. Fucking hypnotic.

"I'm off the sauce." He grinned, head cocked, a quick wink, and one hand pulling out a small white packet of what I assumed to be coke from the inside pocket of his leather jacket.

"And on the skids," I quipped, turning toward the bedroom door, which he quickly pinned me against.

"Don't walk away from me. Not again. I'll leave. I will. Let's just smoke a cigarette, do a little line, and if you want me to leave, I'll go. Promise. I just want to look at you for another five minutes."

He slowly backed away, pulling me with him, easing me onto the couch as he got down on one knee, like a love-struck delinquent, sucking air between his teeth and whispering, "Damn . . . You are a luscious little bitch . . ." He opened the packet, spilled out some powder, rolled a note, and handed it to me with a sweet smile that concealed his deceit and treachery. I had to get the hell away from him or I'd be suckered right back in.

"I need coffee . . ." I lied. I needed to split. "I'll put some on."

I slithered off the couch, fake smile planted on my lips, and suggested he chop out a few fatties. I'd be right back. I planned on spiking him again. I still had half a dozen Seconals left over from our binge in New York. I quit that shit when I quit him. Make it strong enough and black enough and he'll never know what hit him. I'd grab a bag, write a note, and leave both the psychopath and the sociopath where they belonged. In fucking comas.

I could hear the methodical rhythm of razor on glass. A deep snotty inhalation as he cleared his throat. A quick snort followed by a soft chuckle. Why the hell was that motherfucker chuckling? It prickled the hair on the back of my neck.

I poured the coffee, emptied the red devils into the muddy brew, and prayed for deliverance while slinking over to the couch. He handed me the note, I gave him the cup. I just wanted to get this over with.

He swigged the coffee like he was chugging beer. Old habits and all that shit. I snorted a fat blast of what I thought was coke and immediately fell ass backward, landing on the bag I had been packing earlier that night and hitting my head on the edge of the table. It knocked me out.

I woke up bloody and puking. Projectile vomiting. All over the table. All over his dope. All over his boots. Down the front of my slip. Great heaving waves of gelatinous funk shooting out of my mouth and nose. Thick rich fists of sour phlegm cascading in golden arcs all over the room. I pissed myself and started to laugh. The bastard had almost killed me. I had never done heroin. He knew that. It just wasn't my trip. I wasn't looking for nirvana, a velvet womb, or a soft euphoric haze of interstellar space to melt into. I dug the shit that jacked up the irritation level. Barbs and booze. Coke or speed. LSD. Something that accelerated my already jacked-up metabolism. I wasn't interested in slowing shit down. Smoothing it out. Softening the edges. I wanted to keep the edges rough, like the one I had just hit my head against. The one that had finally banged a bit of sense into my thick nugget. Never, under any circumstances, will I ever again answer the door at five forty-five a.m. on a Sunday morning.

Deedee Cheriel

JOHN ALBERT grew up in Los Angeles. As a teenager he cofounded the seminal "death rock" band Christian Death, then played drums for a stint in Bad Religion. He has written for the *Los Angeles Times, LA Weekly, Fader,* and *Hustler,* winning national awards for sports and music writing. His essays have appeared in numerous national anthologies. The film rights to his book *Wrecking Crew,* which chronicles the true-life adventures of an amateur baseball team comprised of drug addicts, transvestites, and washed-up rock stars, have been optioned by the actor Philip Seymour Hoffman.

the monster
by john albert

I wake up to the sound of surf with sand in my mouth. After a few seconds I manage to sit up and focus on my surroundings. I'm underneath a lifeguard stand on a beach just south of the Los Angeles airport. It is dawn so I instinctively check the water. It's smooth as glass with perfectly shaped peaks rolling in. I am wearing a thrift-store suit and suede Hush Puppies. Not exactly the latest in surf wear. As I trudge toward the parking lot, a group of long-haired surfers carrying short dayglo boards approach. They get closer and recognize me.

"Danny, what's up? It's good to see you. Welcome back, dude!"

I force a smile feeling like a has-been. A week ago I turned twenty years old.

Half an hour later I'm nearby in the residential neighborhood I grew up in. It's typical Southern California suburbia: flat houses, dying lawns, and campers. I walk to my parents' front door, reach under a fern, and grab their spare key.

Inside the house is quiet. It's just past dawn and my parents are still asleep. I walk into the kitchen and pour myself a glass of milk. My old cat appears on the counter purring loudly and I scratch his head. I walk down the hallway into my old room and sit on the bed which seems surprisingly small. I remember how safe I felt as a kid and want so badly to go back in time. I don't notice my mom standing in the doorway until she speaks.

"You're home."

I nod and fight an urge to start crying.

"Do you want some breakfast?"

I say yes, but not because I'm hungry. The pills are wearing off and I am starting to feel nauseous. But eating breakfast in my parents' kitchen seems like it might somehow bring me back to a world less horrific than where I have just been. "I'm gonna wash up," I tell her. "I'll be out in a minute."

In the bathroom I glance in the mirror. My pupils are getting huge from withdrawal. I notice something dark in my hair, pick it out, and inspect it. It is congealed blood. I drop it in the toilet and the water clouds red. I immediately slide a small plastic bottle from my pocket, shake out the two remaining pills, and dump them in as well. I am done.

A day before, I'm wearing the same suit and feeling much better. I'm sitting on the fold-out bed in my small apartment with five hundred dollars on the coffee table in front of me. That afternoon, my rich young girlfriend left for the desert with a group of our friends. The plan is for me to join them later that night after scoring the necessary narcotics. Ordinarily, with cash in hand, this would take a couple of hours at the most. This afternoon the task is made far more difficult by a citywide police crackdown.

In the last month there has been a series of home invasion—style robberies in the wealthy Westside neighborhoods. Victims have been violently assaulted in their beautiful homes, sometimes even sexually, their valuables stolen. What really set the world on tilt was when the perpetrators busted into the home of world-famous actress Betty Le Mat. The grand dame is well into her seventies, her classic roles distant history, but she remains a beloved figure and cultural icon. Beyond merely robbing the regal old lady, rumors have been circulating about a particularly gruesome sexual assault involving her cherished "best actress" Oscar statuette.

In response, the entire police force is prowling the streets day and night in a collective rage, clamping down on anything remotely illegal. They are making arrests by the thousands, packing the already overflowing jails in an effort to gain information from anyone willing to talk in exchange for freedom. As a direct result, every respectable drug dealer has either been arrested or has decided to visit out-of-town relatives.

So here I am—money in hand, tapping my feet, racked with nervous twitchy energy, and working the phones. I've been calling everyone I can think of who might know where to score. So far it's been a unanimous chorus of no's accompanied by a lot of sniffling noses and junkie whining. To combat my own withdrawals I've been swallowing some codeine pills I stole from my dad's medicine cabinet last time I visited my dear parents. While not in full dry heave withdrawals, I'm not exactly comfortable either. That said, the pile of cash in front of me makes the world a more hopeful place.

My persistence pays off and I get a serious lead. A once famous singer of a now defunct hair metal band says he scored some overpriced Persian the night before. The deal was facilitated by an older record executive turned cokehead we both casually know. Without saying goodbye I hang up and make the call.

Twenty minutes later I'm getting buzzed into a large art deco apartment building just off a seedy stretch of Hollywood Boulevard. Not waiting for the elevator I scurry up several flights of stairs and arrive at a door where a shirtless tanned man in his sixties named Ron lets me into a spacious apartment. Behind him stands a far-too-thin, forty-something woman named Ann whose ravaged beauty perfectly mimics the fading grandeur of the building. The two have obviously been on a cocaine binge. Ron is sweating and talking a mile a minute about music. He used to be a big shot in the business and keeps dropping names of new bands he thinks will impress me. I really don't give a shit. This kind of chatter is strictly a coke thing and I find it annoying.

The buzzer finally rings; the connection has arrived. He's a thin Persian kid in his early twenties, dressed kind of new wave. He appears as jittery as the other two, avoiding eye contact and laughing at nothing in particular. The three seem to know one another so I hand over my cash. I will wait there while he gets the dope and brings it back. It's something I would never do on the street, but a mutual friend's apartment is another story.

He doesn't come back. Initially I tell myself he's just late like every other power-drunk dealer. I eventually persuade Ron to call him but there's no answer. To placate me Ron and his girl offer some cocaine. I know it will only exasperate my withdrawals, but I still say yes. I just need drugs. After the rush it makes things worse. No surprise. After several more hits I am crawling out of my skin and so desperate for heroin that I feel like I can kill.

"Fuck you guys!" I suddenly roar at Ron and his girlfriend. "You were in on this the whole time. *You're* fucking responsible."

"We had no idea!" Ron's girlfriend yells back, with shrill indignation. "See what happens when you get involved with junkies? Just get the fuck out of here!"

I skulk toward the door, stop, and turn back. "You're responsible" I repeat, pointing an accusatory finger at them both. "This isn't over!"

I step outside and the sun is already up. As I walk back to my car I am absolutely seething. The whole thing is made immensely worse by my increasing need for heroin. The world now appears too bright and everything looks ugly. With the cash gone my options are severely limited and I point the car once again for my parents' house. Maybe my dad has left his pain pills in their usual hiding place. Forty minutes later I walk out of their house with the remaining four pills. It should last me a few hours at best. I drive and try to think of who might still be willing to loan me some money. It's a nonexistent list. I decide to get some alcohol to take the edge off and pull into a liquor store. As I climb out I see a familiar figure leaning against the wall, lighting a cigarette, and I get an idea I will come to regret.

Troy Galt is the most frightening person I know. He is enormous, well over six-foot-five, and built like a professional football player, which is what he would have become if he hadn't gone off to war. He has a thick beard that makes him look far older than his twenty-two years and he is undeniably insane. Not the kind of crazy where he directs traffic with a potted plant on his head— the kind where he will cripple someone and then calmly wash the blood from his hands. If that isn't enough, Troy has a metal plate in his head. He took a bullet to the dome while butchering some enemy combatants in close quarters. It seems the army approved of the deed but not his methods—which reportedly involved a decapitation. He was awarded an honorable discharge and came home to wander the streets and sleep on the beaches of his previous life.

Troy and I went to school together from elementary up to high school. Even as a kid Troy wasn't exactly a pacifist and was capable of beating the shit out of anyone who challenged him. But after several years doing unspeakable things in the Special Forces, he seemed a different species

"How's it going?" I ask, climbing out of my car.

He studies me and furrows his brow. "Hey, dude," he says. "I want some heroin. You have any?"

I shake my head. "I should have a whole bunch of good dope, but some fucking dude burned me last night."

"Robbed you?"

"Listen, man, if you help me get my dope back, half of it is yours. Interested?"

He smiles weirdly like he's amused and I'm certain he's going to tell me to get lost. Unfortunately he doesn't. "I'll get your dope back," he says, and flicks his cigarette against my car.

We arrive back at the Hollywood apartment building and grab the door as a tanned actor type is walking out. He starts to object, sees Troy, and keeps moving. Upstairs, an irritated and still shirtless Ron opens the door thinking it is just me. I see concern in his eyes when Troy follows in behind me.

I calmly ask if there have been any new developments. Before he can answer his girlfriend walks into the room, her eyes wild from the cocaine.

Who the fuck is this?" she says, gesturing wildly at Troy.

"This is my friend. Half the money was his."

"Don't even try it, asshole!" she screams at me.

Ron shoots her a look to shut up. She either doesn't notice or doesn't care. "We're not scared of you and your fucking goon here," she continues. "I know people that will eat you two for fucking lunch. Get the hell out of here before I make a call."

I'm thinking of a proper response when there's a flash of movement to my side. I turn and see Ron crumpled on the floor with Troy looming over him.

"Hey!" the girl yells out, and begins to scramble for the phone. Troy picks up a floor lamp and throws it like a javelin. It hits her in the face and she drops to her knees with a groan. She brings her hands to her mouth and blood trickles out through her fingers. I am stunned by the sudden violence. Fantasies are one thing, but to actually see people hurt is something entirely different. I stand there as if in shock.

Troy studies me a beat. "Why don't you go wait in the car, dude," he says.

I nod and start for the door.

"Hey," he calls after me. I look back. "Don't you fucking drive off," he says, staring at me as a warning.

I sit in my little car with my head just spinning. I have made a serious mistake. I think about calling the police and try to envision the various outcomes. When I finally make up my mind to call, the passenger door swings open and Troy slides in. He hands me a slip of paper with a handwritten address. There is blood smeared on it.

"Are those two still alive?" I ask, my heart pounding so hard I can feel it in my ears.

Troy lights a cigarette, expressionless. I notice blood on his knuckles. "They'll live," he replies. "Let's go."

We drive west on Santa Monica Boulevard in silence. The streets are crawling with cop cars. An hour ago I would have been frightened by them. Now I have to fight the urge to flag one down. The address takes us to an expensive-looking modern apartment building a block off Westwood Boulevard in the Little Tehran neighborhood. As the two of us walk into the mirrored lobby, I decide to speak up.

"I don't want any more violence, Troy. Maybe we can just scare the dude a little. He didn't seem very tough."

Troy stares at me blankly, like a dog trying to read a novel. "Why do you hate violence so much?" he asks sincerely.

"Because it's fucking ugly," I respond.

"The world is ugly. Always has been. Go back and read your history books." He presses the elevator button and pulls a large military knife from his pant leg. "I'm going to do whatever the situation calls for."

"And what if they have a gun, then what?"

"Oh well . . ."

We exit the elevator and count door numbers till we arrive at the unit. The door has been left open slightly which seems odd.

Troy just walks in. I stand there, terrified. When I don't hear anything I head in after him. I see Troy standing in a living room, fish-
ing a butterscotch candy out of a jar. I walk in to join him and get
a surge of adrenalin. There on the floor is the young heroin dealer
who ripped me off. He has a very noticeable bullet wound in his
stomach. His eyes are open and blinking.

"Oh shit, he's shot?!" I exclaim, my voice shaking. I have
never seen someone this seriously injured in my life.

"Yep," Troy responds, sucking on the candy.

"We have to call an ambulance."

"He'll be dead before they get here," Troy explains calmly.

It suddenly occurs to me that the guy on the floor is listening
to us. Before I can say anything, Troy takes a knee, leans close,
and talks to him: "I'm not gonna bullshit you—we can't help you,
you are gonna die here, and that's a fact. But there is something I
can do for you. Tell me who killed you and stole your dope, and I
promise I will make them pay for what they did."

The guy stares up at Troy and I'm not sure he understands.
Then he speaks in a dry-mouthed whisper: "Nazis . . . The Snake
Pit . . ."

.

The Snake Pit is a located across Pacific Coast Highway from Topanga State Beach at the southern end of Malibu. It is hidden away
in a brush-filled canyon and only accessible by a narrow winding
dirt road. There are about ten old bungalows there, nearly all of
them submerged into the ground so people have to enter through
the second story. It's the result of near constant flooding over several decades and has left the once sought after real estate a den of
drugs and fringe dwellers. Both Troy and I have been there on different occasions, both to buy drugs. In my case it was a month ago
when I spent a sketched-out night waiting for some heroin with
two Nazi greaser types, one of them holding a baby.

As we drive up the coast, I ask Troy what his plan is. He pauses so long I think he's not going to answer. Then he does, kind of. "We're going to go in there and get our drugs. Then you're going to leave and I am going to fuck shit up."

I can't help but let out a short laugh. The situation seems surreal. "These guys we're going to see? These are some hardcore penitentiary peckerwoods. I'm thinking they're gonna be ready for us."

Troy smiles. "Definitely."

"I don't suppose you would consider not going?"

"We're gonna finish this."

Troy and I sit on some crumbling steps leading down to the beach across the highway from the Snake Pit. We are waiting for darkness, staring out at the waves, surfers visible in silhouette.

"You miss it?" I ask him, nodding to the surf. "You were good."

"Nah," Troy responds. "That ain't me anymore."

"It could be again."

"There ain't nothing good left in me."

"What do you mean?"

"I was never a saint, I know that. But I'm not even human anymore." He taps his forehead. "Shit is broken."

"Maybe it's just gonna take some time . . . Dude, let's just go home. We don't need to go on with this. I'll find another way to get us some dope."

"It's not about that, never was." He stands up. "Besides, I promised that dead kid I would get him some justice. If nothing else, I am a man of my word."

It is night and we are down in the Snake Pit. Troy waits behind in a tree line as I walk up to a ramshackle house and knock on a window that now serves as a door. The plan is for me to tell them

I want to buy some more heroin and see who is inside. But before I am even ready, the door swings open and I am pulled inside. Someone shoves me to the ground and kicks me in the ribs. "Stay down!" a rough voice orders.

I eventually roll over and manage a glance around. There is a muscular convict type with greased-back hair and a cowboy mustache standing over me. The small room is filled with expensive goods: jewelry, high-end electronics, fur coats. And there, on a nearby table next to some used syringes and a pistol, is Betty Le Mat's gleaming Oscar. The sudden realization that I have found the guys doing the home invasions is instantly followed by the understanding that they will surely kill me.

One of the Nazi greasers I met there before walks in and looks at me. He is shirtless—the words *South Bay* tattooed across his stomach—and holding a large revolver. His eyes have a crystal meth intensity. "I remember you," he says, then nods to the others. "Take him into the bathroom and stick him. Make sure to hold him over the bathtub when he bleeds out."

South Bay starts to light a Camel nonfilter when a figure looms behind him. It is Troy. He reaches forward and moves a knife across the man's throat. A mist of blood sprays out and the guy stumbles forward. His gun goes off making a popping noise. As the other greasers scramble for their weapons, I dive behind a couch. The room erupts into complete chaos as men shout and shoot off guns.

I hear a crashing noise and one of the Nazis falls beside me on the floor and starts convulsing. With a new burst of adrenalin I stand and bolt through the house toward what I hope is a back door. I race through a kitchen area and out another makeshift door into the surrounding trees. As I move away, there is high-pitched screaming unlike anything I have ever heard.

I frantically claw my way up a hillside on my hands and knees.

When I get some distance I finally look back. The house below is now on fire. There are several gunshots and then an eerie silence. I sit there gasping for breath as the house burns. I take out my cell phone and, with trembling hands, call 911. Troy never emerges. No one does. I hear sirens approaching and soon there are emergency lights descending into the darkness of the canyon.

In the ensuing days, a sanitized story of what happened is offered up to the public. News broadcasts tell of a decorated war veteran who lost his life single-handedly taking down an ultra-violent crime ring. And really, that is what happened. The rest is merely context. In my opinion Troy knew he couldn't exist in the civilized world anymore so he went out doing something he thought was noble. Beyond the fact that he had become a monster, my friend rescued the city.

And in the end he saved my life as well. I was literally scared straight by my day with Troy and have been clean since. That night I left the Snake Pit and drove south along the coast, eventually falling asleep on my local beach, curled up beneath the very same lifeguard stand I had slept under as a clear-eyed kid waiting to surf the dawn patrol. I held onto the sand with an anguished desperation, listening to the waves and willing myself back into a less horrific world.

Robin Doyno

GARY PHILLIPS has edited and contributed to several Akashic Books anthologies, including *The Cocaine Chronicles*, which he coedited with Jervey Tervalon. Recent work includes *The Rinse*, a graphic novel about a money launderer; the novel *The Warlord of Willow Ridge*; and *Treacherous: Grifters, Ruffians and Killers*, a collection of his short stories. For information, visit www.gdphillips.com.

black caesar's gold
by gary phillips

He had a dream, but it would have made Martin Luther King, Jr. shake his head woefully, Malcolm X tongue lash him severely, and Stokely Carmichael would have pimp slapped him. Frank Matthews, along with the other Frank, Lucas, and Leroy "Nicky" Barnes were, for a time, the kingpins of the heroin trade on the East Coast. Matthews, the self-styled Black Caesar, was a country boy like Lucas. But once he got to the big city, he went all in. Maybe Barnes could quote *Moby-Dick* and *King Lear*, but ascending from juvenile chicken thief in his native Durham to numbers runner in Philadelphia to becoming the first major drug lord in Harlem, Matthews had built an organization his compatriots admired and the Mob feared.

"That moulie's getting too damn big for that mink coat he struts around in," Godfather Joe Bonanno was want to observe.

For Matthews moved product like no other, a Robin Hood in the community and a terror outside of it. Unlike other smaller pushers in Harlem and beyond, he didn't rely on La Cosa Nostra to keep him supplied—as generally speaking, they controlled the pipeline. Matthews had a direct South American connection and brought in H and coke that way, cutting out the usual middleman. He invested in property under various fronts and had cash couriered overseas into tax havens.

One time in Atlanta, Matthews brought together a roomful of big swingin'-dick black and Latino drug dealers to form a combine so as to chill the growing static with the Italian mobsters. Matthews was a strategic motherfucker.

Like Barnes and Lucas, the high-flying Matthews eventually got his wings clipped and was busted by agents of the then newly constituted Drug Enforcement Administration. But different than those two, he didn't rat out his peers for a reduction of his sentence. Then again, Matthews didn't do time in the slammer, either. He liked to gamble in Vegas, these trips also a way for him to launder more of his money.

As these things happen, he had been in Vegas at the time with a beauty on his arm, losing at the craps tables but not sweating it. His plan was to soon be on his way to LA to catch Super Bowl VII between the Redskins and Dolphins. Yet unbeknownst to him, members of his South American network, along with a lieutenant, had already been arrested. The trap was closing in on him, and at McCarran Airport the DEA slapped the cuffs on Matthews and his lady friend.

"What took you so long?" he was quoted as saying jauntily.

Incredibly, his lawyer successfully argued for his bail reduction, at which point Matthews got out of jail and then disappeared. That was 1973. From Chicago to Rome, Nigeria to Atlanta, sightings of Matthews abounded. But none of them panned out. He was never found. Maybe the Mafia had him whacked or maybe Matthews had his face changed and retired to some island with a woman who liked to wear miniskirts and no underwear.

Chuck Grayson pondered Frank Matthews's fate and history as he pretended not to fawn over the too-sweet 1969 Mustang Fastback with a Boss 420 engine. Grayson had done his homework and knew less than a thousand of these particular Mustangs were produced that year. There must have been modifications to the engine compartment to accommodate the larger motor, he mused. A woman in stylish clothes and a wide-brimmed sun hat preceded him from the parking lot where several vehicles were on display.

Along with other potential buyers, they reentered the main room of Stedler and Sons Auctioneers. There was a photo of the maroon Mustang tacked to a padded board with its order in the auction noted. There were other pictures of various items pinned there as well, including vases and an ivory-inlaid cigar box said to have belonged to President Grover Cleveland.

Grayson had come to the auction house because this particular Mustang had belonged to Frank Matthews. Stedler and Sons listed the car as having belonged to Ken Schmecken, a producer and shadowy part owner of three X-rated movie theaters in the Los Angeles area. Grayson was something of a Matthews aficionado and always on the lookout for items connected to the gangster. He knew that *Schmecken*, an oblique slang term for heroin, was one of the names the drug lord had used in hiding his investments.

Because the car had value as being only one of a limited number, there were several interested parties contending for it when it came up for bid. But Grayson was something of a limited edition himself.

He was a mid-thirties African American male who'd made his money as part of a start-up online entity that got sold for a nice profit to a conglomerate controlling various commercial websites. He and his friends' site was one of the first catering to the multicultural geek crowd in all things pop culture, lifestyles, and fashion. Turned out people-of-color dweebs, a group of which Grayson was proudly a member, liked to hang together.

The car cost him more than he would have liked to pay. This was due to the woman across the room in the hat who kept upping him. But she'd dropped out when the asking price went past $25,000. One, two . . . the third strike of the gavel sounded and Grayson would soon possess the vehicle.

The Mustang was found in Altadena in the garage of a house belonging to a long-retired Department of Water and Power secretary named Deborah Keyson. She'd died of pulmonary failure, and any connection she may have had to Frank Matthews or Ken Schmecken was not known.

The auctioneers had put money into restoring the car and it had been fairly well-preserved under a tarp, the gas and fluids having been drained from it back when. Grayson had chanced upon its photo and description while sitting in his dentist's office paging through a freshly minted Stedler and Sons catalogue. He immediately recognized the name Schmecken in the brief write-up.

The paperwork done and money deposited, Grayson drove his prize away from the auction house in Glendale. He couldn't help but imagine he was Matthews at the wheel on his way to cement a nefarious deal as he drove home to Santa Monica. Along the way his phone rang and he answered, putting it on speaker and propping it in the opening of the car's built-in ashtray.

"So?" his girlfriend Mora Fleming asked.

"Scored it, sweeite."

"I knew you would."

"Yeah, well."

"Want me to bring Chinese or Indian?"

"I could go for some kung pao chicken."

She chuckled. "When do you *not* want that?"

"I want you."

"Hmmmm. See you soon."

Fleming, without her heavy boots on, was two inches taller than Grayson and outweighed his wiry frame by forty pounds— forty solid pounds. She was a bodybuilding chiropractor and gaming enthusiast. They'd met at the annual Nexus of Nerds— Comic-Con in San Diego. She'd come with a girlfriend, a fellow bodybuilder, and they'd turned the heads of fanboys and their put-upon fathers—the two of them dressed in the fantasy of scantily clad sword-wielding barbarian women.

Standing in line to get into a panel with comics superstar writer Neil Gaiman, Fleming had been impressed with Grayson's knowledge of the *S.T.A.R. Ops* game in phantom mode. That, and he managed to look at her face and not just her substantial chest.

In bed later, cuddling after making love to Fleming in his second-floor bedroom, Grayson saw through the slats of the window the light over his garage snap on. The light was motion sensitive and normally it coming on meant one of his neighbors' cats was lazing by. But the Mustang was parked in the driveway, near the garage door. He hadn't outfitted the car with an alarm yet, though he'd put a lock bar on the steering wheel.

Grayson waited for the sound of the vehicle's door being opened. He smiled, realizing he better wake up his girlfriend if there was trouble. But the light went off again and there were no more sounds of disturbance from below.

The following morning he was changing out the battery in the trunk when Fleming asked, "Why the heck is it back here?"

"They needed all the room up front to squeeze in the big block engine," Grayson explained, lifting the battery out. He figured the auction house had spent money on the car's looks but not on a more heavy-duty battery. He intended to not scrimp when it came to his new beauty. He was going to use his electric motor Leaf and go to the auto parts store to trade this battery in for a better one. There was a recessed metal shell that held the battery in its cavity. He removed the housing to inspect it for rust.

"What's this?" Fleming asked, reaching a hand into the cavity in the trunk's floorboard. She worked for a few moments undoing some tape and held aloft a plastic sandwich baggie that had been secured on the frame below the battery's shell.

The couple exchanged a look of anticipation as Fleming tore the aged baggie apart and removed a sheet of yellowed paper. Gingerly she unfolded the stiff note and flattened it on the slope of the car's fastback. On the paper was a sentence in block lettering: *SIXTY YARDS NORTH FROM THE PANZER.*

"Panzer?" Fleming asked. "Like German for tank?"

"Precisely," Grayson said, heading for the house. "Let me check something, but I think we might have a road trip this morning."

"Yeah, where?"

"Why, a bombed-out French village, my dear."

The village had gone by various names and had been used in TV shows and movies several times. It was a World War II–era set in Canyon Country that by the late '60s had become mired in an ownership battle between its original builder and the children of one of the ex-partners. This made it difficult to rent out. But in 1970, the village was utilized illegally—that is, the producers didn't bother to pay—for a hardcore shoot called *Madam Satan of the SS*.

"You've seen this epic?" Fleming asked.

"Way before I had the pleasure of your acquaintance. In fact, there was a sequel but that one took place in a mad scientist's castle. Same woman played Madam Satan both times, Jackie Salvo."

"Uh-huh."

"Of course I only know this due to my research into the wild and varied career of Frank Matthews."

"Of course."

Grayson had recalled that under the Ken Schmecken alias, Matthews had been a producer of a porno set during World War II. He'd confirmed this in a nonfiction book he had at home about twentieth-century gangsters which featured an extensive chapter on the disappeared drug lord.

Fleming wondered aloud, "Does *heron*, to use the vernacular of the day, retain its potency over decades?"

"You figure that's what he has buried there?"

She regarded the freeway outside the rolled-down passenger window. The Mustang didn't have air-conditioning. "You think he buried money?"

"He was a careful dude, Mora. Maybe he was planning in case he had to go on the run and needed to make sure he had enough liquid assets to make a break to Mexico or the Bahamas."

She leaned over and kissed him on the cheek. "My little Scarface."

He squeezed her muscular thigh. "Better know it."

Canyon Country was in Santa Clarita, in the northwest section of LA County. In the last twenty years the area had seen the proliferation of housing subdivisions, but there were still large swaths of underpopulated nature. Using tax records and past articles he'd accessed online, Grayson had obtained the location for the place most commonly called Attack Squad Village, as the set had been used several times in the popular 1960s World War II TV show *Attack Squad.*

Once there, they parked and walked along a dusty street bordered by French-style buildings of the proper vintage, a bombed-out church, and a bar called Millie Marie's among the façades. There was another street, then behind the false front of an apartment building, in the tall weeds, they found the German tank.

"North is this way," Fleming said. Each carried shovels. Using a tape measure and allowing for human error, they marked off 180 feet from the tank. Grayson used the point of the shovel to scribe a large circle in the dirt.

Fleming nodded and got started. He began in another section inside the circle. In less than fifteen minutes they'd uncovered a coffin.

"Wow," Fleming intoned. "I didn't expect that."

"We've come this far," he said. They dug the dirt out from around the coffin and together hefted it above ground.

"Damn!" Fleming exclaimed, sweat on her brow.

"Here goes," Grayson said. He used the shovel to lift the lid and let it flop open.

"Oh shit!" Fleming rasped.

Inside the coffin were bricks of gold. Grayson picked up a bar, assessing its weight in his hand—roughly two pounds, he estimated. "How is this possible?" he wondered aloud.

"Gold is good anywhere, Chuck," Fleming observed.

"I got that, but it's illegal to own gold bars."

Hands on her hips, she said, "A drug lord isn't worried about the rules, honey."

"I know that, but what foundry would cast these for him?"

"I can answer that," a new voice said.

The two looked around to find three newcomers, two men in sport coats and slacks, flanking a slender woman in a loose top, white jeans, and heels. She wore a feathered and beaded Mardi Gras eye mask. The two men had on pedestrian ski masks. One of the men, slimmer than the other, pointed a semiauto pistol-grip shotgun at Grayson. A slight wind blew but the couple didn't notice the breeze.

"How'd you know to find us here?" Grayson asked.

The shotgun man snorted. "Like that purple car is hard to follow."

"What you need to worry about," the woman interjected, "is how you're going to pace yourself loading my goods." There was a trace of an accent in her voice.

The smile below her mask was brittle, like a robot trying to be chummy. Grayson, who figured she was the one in the wide-brimmed hat at the auction, noted a mole to the left of her plump lips. The lines on her face indicated a woman of some years, though clearly fit.

The shotgun still on Grayson, the stockier thug retrieved a

white van and backed it close to the loot. He opened the rear swing doors. Resigned, Grayson and Fleming loaded the ingots into the rear cargo area. There were 124 bars.

"Now what?" Grayson said, using the heel of his hand to wipe sweat from his brow. The temperature had risen past the mid-eighties.

"Now we say bye-bye," the woman answered triumphantly.

Fleming was standing near the rear of the van, at an angle to the shotgun holder. She rushed at the man, hoping to tackle him and relieve him of his weapon. But he was a pro and wasn't rattled.

"Back that ass up, you big bitch," he said, clubbing her with the pistol-grip end of the shotgun.

Fleming went down heavy.

"Mora!" Grayson blared, rushing to aid her. The larger hood produced a stun device and jammed it against Grayson's neck. He convulsed and spittle coated his lips as he too dropped to the ground on his knees. A second jolt toppled him and he lay twitching, his muscles unresponsive to his commands. He wet himself.

"That's a cherry ride you got, bro," the one who'd shocked him said. "I'll look good driving that bad boy." The hood removed the keys from Grayson's pocket, easily knocking aside the other man's hand in his feeble attempt to stop the thug.

"Is that necessary?" the woman said.

"It's a perk, baby," the man shot back. He and the shotgunner laughed harshly. The woman said something in Spanish, and the three left in the two vehicles.

Mora Fleming moaned and rolled onto her side. She then got herself up and helped Grayson to his feet.

"That was exciting," she said dryly.

"How're you feeling?" Tenderly, he placed the flat of his hand on the side of her face.

She touched the back of her head. "Some painkillers and intravenous tequila ought to remedy the situation."

He looked beyond her. "I hate getting beat," he declared. "Not to mention, that was a serious haul of gold. And that bastard took my car."

"Maybe we should be happy to be alive, Chuck."

He had an odd smile on his face when he addressed her. It wasn't an expression she'd seen before. "Maybe they shouldn't have left me alive."

Despite him just standing there with the front of his jeans dark from urine, Fleming got nervous.

There were hardly any photos of Frank Matthews aside from booking shots. But Grayson found one of him at a club in Harlem taken by the black-owned *Amsterdam News*, as the white press at that point didn't know who he was. Using a magnifying glass, Grayson studied the picture that showed Matthews smoking a cigar, holding court with a tableful of cohorts. Because it was a close-in shot, not all the faces were distinct. He wonderd if there were other shots from the club.

Via the online records of the New York Public Library, Grayson was able to narrow his possibles to two photographers who worked for the *News* then and who might have taken the uncredited shot. One was dead, and the other, Tim "Cheaters" Pleasy, was still alive. He was seventy-six and taught an extension photography class in Sarasota. Grayson promptly got him on the phone.

"Yeah," Pleasy said after the exchange of pleasantries, his voice clear and young sounding. "Ol' Frank fancied himself the big shot all right. Passing out twenties to the kids on the streets like free lunch, buying color TVs for the senior center . . . Yeah, he was something."

Grayson let the old timer drone on some, then asked, "You

remember a shot you might have taken of him at the Montreaux Club? Him at a table of people having a good time?" He described the scene in further detail.

"Naw, young man, that don't ring no bell," Cheaters Pleasy said. "I'd bet Garmes took that shot." Davis Garmes was the deceased photographer.

"Any idea where his outtakes got to? He have family? I wanted to see if he had other shots showing the faces clearly."

"You sure seem to want to go through a lot for your book," Pleasy observed.

"I might have an uncle in that shot, and I want to know for certain," he lied.

"I got you," the older man said. "I'll check on that and will get back to you. I might know where some of his old photos went."

"That would be great, Mr. Pleasy."

It didn't take the photographer long, as he and the late Garmes had stayed in touch. He was able to locate the man's photos left in the possession of an ex-wife he also knew. Garmes's photos were in various film boxes designated by years. She found two other shots Garmes had taken that night, had them scanned, and eventually they reached Grayson via e-mail.

"There she is," Grayson said to Fleming. They sat at his kitchen island. He tapped the magnifying glass against his opposite hand. "That beauty mark, mole, whatever you want to call it, gives her away. She's at the table here with Matthews."

Fleming folded her arms. "And she's the one playing Madam Satan in those two pornos he produced?"

"Yep. Jackie Salvo, but that's an alias."

Fleming frowned. "Okay, let's say you find out her real name, which isn't hard, then what?"

"Get our shit back."

She put a hand on his. "Darling, we go see action-adventure movies and read comic books. But unfortunately, I'm not Wonder Woman and you aren't the Punisher."

He winked. "But we've role-played them."

"I'm serious, Chuck. This woman ain't playing."

"We've handled guns," he countered.

"Shooting targets at a firing range isn't the same thing as blasting a human being, and you know it. We might be geekazoids but we're solid citizens, baby. We pay taxes, have businesses, homes—in other words, unless you're willing to give all that up, I say drop this."

"Let me just identify her. Just that, for my own satisfaction."

She folded her arms again, a questioning look to her. "Don't think you're slick."

"Me? Never."

Finding out the real name of a woman who starred in two X-rated cult movies from the '70s was easier than buttoning a shirt. Once he had that information, Grayson was able to document the up-and-down career of Pilar Ortega Renaud De La Fontana. She'd gained notoriety back then from the Madam Satan films and graduated to starring in a few grade-C horror and sci-fi movies. She had some TV roles too, and in the '90s hosted a cable access show where she made smart-ass remarks and one-liners throughout whatever turkey she was showing.

Naturally, there were a couple of fan clubs devoted to her among nerd-dom, and getting an address for the woman wasn't too tough either, given Grayson knew who to ask what. At a coffee shop on Olympic Boulevard, he met with a man who De La Fontana twice had imposed a restraining order against.

"It's not like I meant her any harm," said Fred Summerville, an underemployed box store clerk. He nibbled on the second Rice Krispies treat Grayson had bought him.

Grayson sized up Summerville as the type who got off on some peep action, and heaven would be sniffing De La Fontana's panties. But he said, "I feel you, man, where would these celebs be if it wasn't for us keeping their names out there?"

"Exactly," Summerville agreed happily, bits of his treat exploding from his mouth.

More commiserating included Summerville warning Grayson about a fifty-some-odd-old boyfriend of De La Fontana named Boris who'd done time for strong arm robbery. He didn't know the last name of this bruiser, but what the restraining orders couldn't do, Boris had done when he'd come into Summerville's store and calmly broken his hand.

"I stayed away after that," the former stalker stated flatly, looking down.

The $150 in cash Grayson offered elevated the man's mood and produced an address. She lived in a modest Craftsman in East Hollywood not too far from the large Kaiser medical facility on Sunset and Vermont.

On the second night of his stakeout in his Leaf, Grayson saw the Mustang arrive and a stocky man in his fifties exit the vehicle and enter the house.

Fleming was right. Grayson wasn't about to storm in there armed with an AK, a bandanna tied around his head, demanding the gold and his car back. But he'd be damned if he was going to get taken advantage of and not do something. Driving back to Santa Monica, he came up with a plan and discussed it with his girlfriend the next day in her office.

"Oh, man," she said finally. "That's a shitty idea, Chuck."

"It could work."

"Or we could spend several years in prison, if we don't get killed. And if it's the former, I couldn't stand the thought of a booty bandit wearing out that fine ass of yours."

"Good to know," he said. "Anyway, it's not we, just me."

"Bullshit. He's my patient and you're not doing this without my help. Besides, I don't want you going to the next con talking about how I pussied out on you."

They both grinned broadly.

Grayson wanted to obtain a kilo of black tar heroin—those tense opening teasers of many a *Miami Vice* of cool crooks and sweating undercover cops flashing through his mind. He owned the complete box set on DVD. But trying to buy that kind of weight also meant making connections beyond Fleming's patient. And this meant gaining the acquaintance of certain individuals who'd cut out your intestines and sell them back to you as a scarf. So he settled for two small glassine packets with a blue devil head stenciled on them.

The patient Fleming was treating for back alignment problems was very much into holistic health and organic foods, which he gladly talked about extensively. Yet when you work on a person's body up close and personal like she did, the conversing invariably covered a lot of territory—like one's past.

Todd Jessup, the patient, had been a pharmacist who got hooked on the drugs he dispensed. He lost his license and in his descent, encountered various unsavory individuals. He'd subsequently rebuilt his life, and it took some coaxing but he came up with a few contacts from the bad old days. Thereafter, Grayson and Fleming bought the blue devil packets from a hard-ass runaway teenager working for her pusher-pimp boyfriend in the Valley. The one-time pharmacist verified the authenticity of the packets' contents.

Staging the accident came next. Boris no-last-name was driving the Mustang back to De La Fontana's house from the Vons supermarket, blasting the Eagles on the aftermarket CD unit.

Grayson almost cried as he purposely bashed his Leaf into the left front fender of the classic vehicle. Boris was out in a shot, yelling.

"The fuck is wrong with you, man? You blind or something? Hey, it's you," he said, recognizing Grayson.

"Your mama's blind, bitch," Grayson responded.

Boris rushed over and Grayson jabbed him in the face without hesitation. This earned him a left to the stomach and a right to the chin. He was younger than Boris by more than twenty years, but the other man was far more experienced with his fists.

"What, figured you'd try and get your car back, punk? Well come on."

He laughed and again hit Grayson, who rocked back; he ducked the next blow but the inevitable was upon him. A crowd gathered, cheering the combatants. By the time the motorcycle cop arrived, there was a cell phone video of Grayson getting his ass kicked up on YouTube. Though at one point, down on all fours, Grayson had managed to get ahold of his tormentor's calf and bite through his pant leg. A couple of people watching clapped at that.

As Boris Stallings had no paperwork for the Mustang, nor proof of insurance, the car was impounded and searched. Stallings was arrested for possession of heroin, planted under the floor mat on the passenger side by Mora Fleming as her boyfriend took his beatdown. The door had been locked, but when Grayson got the car he'd been given two sets of keys. She'd argued she should be the one to plow into the Mustang as she felt she could handle herself better against Stallings.

"Dammit, woman, you've already seen me piss myself. What pride do I have left?" Grayson had said.

She'd kissed him. "A man must do what he must do."

It took a week to recuperate at home from his encounter with Stallings. His face was still tender. The Santa Monica PD notified

Grayson about his car once LAPD contacted them. Grayson told the police he had been in the area to shop at Skylight Books and was shocked to see the Mustang that had been jacked from him the week before. He'd lost control of the car and that's when this horrible Stallings person went wild on him.

He also saw on the news that De La Fontana had been found shotgunned to death in her house, though no ingots were mentioned. A known associate of Stallings was said to be a person of interest.

Among the online fan club there was talk that De La Fontana had family ties to one of Frank Matthews's South American financiers. It was speculated that she and Mathews had been romantically linked at one point. There was also a rumor about her being the mistress at age seventeen of a general who'd absconded with treasures from his country's coffers.

In a chat room, Grayson read the suggestion that maybe she'd done Matthews in after he ripped her off, and that she must have been on the hunt for the gold for a long time. But her killing him didn't make sense, since she would have needed him alive to reveal where the gold was hidden. Though could be she got carried away having him worked over, someone else offered, and so it went, back and forth. All this merely conjecture among her fans.

Grayson got the Mustang repaired and painted a sedate color. Now and then behind the wheel, Mora Fleming humming to an oldie on the radio beside him, he wondered whatever became of Black Caesar's gold.

Sheila Rose Photography

ANTONIA CRANE is the only person from Humboldt County who doesn't smoke or grow weed. Her work can be found or is forthcoming in the *Rumpus, Black Clock, Slake, PANK,* the *Los Angeles Review of Books,* ŻYŻŻYVA, and elsewhere. She wrote a memoir about her mother's illness and the sex industry, *SPENT,* and is currently seeking representation for that memoir. She teaches incarcerated teenage girls creative writing in Los Angeles. For more information, visit antoniacrane.com.

sunshine for adrienne
by antonia crane

The first man who raped her went blind. Her mom called with the news.

"That handsome football player you dated got eye cancer in both eyes," she said.

Adrienne heard chewing and the wet slurp of Nicorette gum. Her ma chewed two or three pieces at a time and when they lost flavor, she rolled the spit stones into gray balls and stuck them to the kitchen counter. The orange cat knocked them onto the floor and batted them around.

"You mean Terry?" Adrienne's asshole clenched. Ma didn't know. All the girls at St. Julian's High School swooned over Terry's tanned wide receiver chest and tennis legs. She heard something being chopped on a cutting board with a steady *whack, whack, whack.*

"He's blind as a bat. His poor mother." The chopping got faster and faster and more precise. She could slice a carrot into paper-thin pieces in less than thirty seconds. She hated cooking.

"She's a nut job, Amy!" her father hollered in the background. A cupboard door slammed shut. She heard the refrigerator door make a sucking sound as it opened.

Adrienne found her prework hit and bent spoon in the top drawer of her dresser, but no lighter. She rummaged around in another drawer where she last saw it and found ticket stubs from a show her father took her to when she graduated high school. It was the Della Davidson Dance Company's *Ten p.m. Dream*, an interpretation of *Alice in Wonderland*. They'd nibbled calamari beforehand next door. Her football-watching, beer-drinking father even sported a silky burgundy tie that matched her favorite red skirt. She'd taken her father's elbow as he led her to the front row, so close she felt the dancers' abdominal muscles vibrate and their snaky necks glisten and strain. She watched them as he watched the music pulse through her skin.

He liked to look at her pictures of birds too. She'd started drawing turkeys, doves, and chickens when she was six years old with accidental skill. Her father couldn't draw an Easter egg if there was a gun to his head. Where he lacked imagination, she swelled with it. Her talents delighted him and he bragged about her to his roofing buddies. "My daughter's a genius," he'd say while ripping off grubby tiles. He collected her bird drawings and stuck them to the refrigerator door, where they were held in place by 49er magnets.

"Her only son. Can you imagine?" Ma's voice matched the sucking thud the refrigerator door made when it closed.

The thing being chopped was gone and in its place, her father's voice: "Her loser son, still living at home at twenty-nine?" He grunted, which was the same as his laugh.

Adrienne pictured him in his stretched white gym socks with a spaghetti noodle dangling from a fork, daring Ma to slap his hand away from her butt, which he pinched when he wasn't yelling at the TV, drinking Coors Light, with their orange cat on the footstool. The skin on his hands matched his face: tanned, calloused, and flaking off from working outside in the wind, rain, and dense fog that made roofs wet and slippery. He fell off a ladder and sprained his ankle last year. It swelled like a grapefruit so he managed the office and bid jobs, and farmed out the labor to his friends.

It was at St. Julian's High School where Adrienne got sneaky. She'd tiptoe behind him on her way upstairs to her room. She'd been meeting Terry and getting high, staying out past curfew.

"Where the hell you been?" Her father had stopped looking at her. He held the TV remote in one hand, raised like an arrow, in the other, a beer. He was a channel surfer. There had been a steadily growing gulf between them. Her curves brought popularity, lip gloss, tampons, and boys, but also self-righteousness and danger. She became reckless and reticent. He'd hear her whispering on the phone well after midnight. He'd smell alcohol on her breath. She'd become too pretty for her own good, he sensed.

"Where?" he asked. He was made of sounds: slurps, moans, burps, and coughs. Startled, the cat leaped off the footstool and ran into the kitchen. She watched a red river of varicose veins travel up his chubby calves to his thighs. She didn't have to hide her tiny-dot pupils or her droopy, rubbery skin that hung on her face. He watched the football game on TV: "Olson, you pile of shit, you throw like a girl!"

She fingered the box of Marlboros in her pocket.

"I was out buying smokes." She waved the box in the air so he could see it reflected in the TV screen.

"You're too young to smoke."

"I'm seventeen."

"It's eleven o'clock on a school night, Addy." Along with breasts, she'd sprouted a shitty new petulance. Her father disliked the distance between them. He gripped his Coors Light tighter knowing that if he didn't keep engaging with her, she would slip away and it would be too late. Perhaps it was already too late. The amount of rage he felt surprised him.

Adrienne shrugged her shoulders. She walked briskly into the kitchen where her ma buzzed around in slippers, gnashing her gum and talking on the phone aggressively like the women on *The View*.

* * *

The sun dropped into her tenderloin apartment like a dried, rancid apricot, bringing night. She spotted her lighter on the floor next to the trash. She leaned over, swiped, and shook it. It was out of fluid, but when she tried it anyway, a low flame appeared.

"Terry's not a loser. He's ill. How would you like to be blind, hmm?"

"Wow, Ma. That's awful," Adrienne said. The bathroom where she was raped was light blue with no windows. She reached for the soft brown belt on the floor, next to her Lucite stripper shoes. A gray pigeon stood on the single window ledge in her studio apartment. Her hands began to sweat.

"I'm going to bring them my famous broccoli casserole. You should come with me."

Adrienne grabbed the belt and tied it around her forearm. She pulled it taught, gripping it with her teeth. Her best wormy vein surfaced inside her left elbow. The sweat from her hands transferred onto the worn leather where there were tiny dots of blood. She pictured diced sweet yellow onions and the hard shell of orange melted cheese on top. Terry would peel the hard cheese layer off and chew it with his bleached Chiclets. He would shake Ma's hand with his tennis doubles grip.

When he asked about Adrienne, her ma would lie. She'd tell him, "She's waiting tables and taking World Religions at City College." But that was four years ago. It was the story she liked to tell the neighbors. The needle hit the vein nicely and delivered the juicy black heat from Adrienne's belly up to her neck. She levitated from her chest to the top of her head. Butterflies came to mind. She took a dull pencil and drew some on a Post-it.

"If you get on BART now, you can make it in an hour." Her ma's voice turned smoky and silver.

The chopping sound was back but softer, like a slow finger tapping on water in a bowl. *Tap. Tap. Tap.*

"Adrienne, are you still there?" Her cheeks warmed and her eyes drifted like a plant leaning toward sunlight.

"I can't go to Oakland tonight, Ma. I have to work." The space between them stretched far and wide as the Pacific Ocean.

"Come over for dinner tomorrow night. Spend some time with your father."

Ma's breath was heavy and slow like hers. There was no more gum noise. She heard the oven door snap shut and a timer tick. She felt comfort knowing the casserole was inside and the cheese would spread like butter and the chopped broccoli would sizzle, as planned. She heard relief in her ma's mighty exhale. She exhaled too.

"I can't. I have to make rent for this shitty rat-hole apartment."

"Okay, honey. We'll see you on Sunday."

Adrienne felt elegant and weightless in her tall, thick black motorcycle boots. They were heavier than she was. She chose a fishnet top to cover the purple-red scars that lined her forearms. Her hair was pulled back in a neat, shiny bun. She hadn't washed it in days. When she was high, water felt like nails. Besides, the high rollers liked the tight bun. It read ballerina. Well groomed. Middle class. Her boyfriend Dennis liked it too. "You look like a French lingerie model," he'd said. They lived together in a dinky apartment on Hyde Street where they listened to trance techno music, counted pigeons, and slammed dope. Dennis looked at least forty, with crooked lines around his mouth and creased eyes. But he was twenty-eight, like her.

She checked her mailbox on the way out and found a red envelope from her father. She shoved it in her costume bag and walked the few blocks to Market Street Cinema, past the garbage that blew over the sidewalk and into the gutter. Fog drifted in and circled her like wet smoke. She gave a light wave to the homeless guy who always tried to sell her stolen perfume. Pigeons picked through the trash and carried off chicken bones in their beaks. Three pigeons in the trash can; three grams of dope per day.

On the floor at the MSC, she saw her regular customer, the man in the white shirt, sitting in his usual spot. He was good for a hundred bucks. He sometimes brought her a single red carnation, which she thought was cheap and sad, but she smiled and thanked him and later tossed it into the gutter on Market Street. He glanced at his watch. She climbed over the crossed legs of a guy in a stocking cap, to get to the man in the white shirt. A familiar hand touched her bare stomach as she walked by.

"Sorry."

She bent in half to lean in for a closer look. Dennis had a swollen, bruised eye that she could see, even in the dark, and he was bleeding from one corner of his mouth.

"What are you doing at my work?"

The white-shirt customer now had a thick blonde gyrating on his crotch. Timing is everything.

"I was trying to bring you . . ."

"What?"

Dennis uncrossed his legs. His fingers were long and graceful. He hid his face in his hands. Adrienne leaned in and hissed in his ear. He smelled like bleach, dirt, and night. His eyes were badly swollen.

"You are never supposed to come into my work."

"I need . . ." Adrienne peeled his hands away from his face and remembered the birthday card from her father. She had torn open the envelope and found eighty dollars. He'd written, *Hope Your Birthday is Ducky*, on top of a picture of a fluffy green duck she drew when she was about nine years old. It was her "duck phase," her father liked to remind her.

She smashed forty crisp dollars into Dennis's sweaty palm. A leggy redhead whispered to a customer next to him, then glanced in her direction. It was obvious they were arguing, and it was making customers tense. The white-shirt customer smiled at her. She smiled big. She smiled rectus. She smiled Cheshire. The vein in Dennis's neck bulged, the same way it did when he came. She moved her chest up to his bruised eyes, like she was about to dance for him.

"Get the fuck out of my work."

The white-shirt customer motioned to her to come over to him. She walked over and leaned in to kiss his cheek. Most nights, after work, Dennis took her money and met their dealer. Then they got high together and Dennis played guitar on their dingy brown sheets.

"Promise me you'll never come into my work," she said.

"Promise."

The numbers were good at the MSC. She gave five or eight handjobs a night and left with seven or eight hundred bucks, enough for six grams. If she only did her share, she and Dennis could stay blazed for a couple days. The next night, she'd come back to work and do it again. And the next day the exact same thing. Never mind the bruises on the backs of her knees. She felt light and graceful on stage. Six years of ballet as a little girl kept her toes pointed and her arms loose. And there was her techno trance music where she got lost on stage.

She had three songs to get naked. The first one was frantic and unrelenting. She walked on stage slow as caramel, traveling to the side. Back and forth. When the beat got faster, she slowed down even more, pulling her shadow across the length of the stage toward the pole. She grabbed it with one hand and slid down to the floor. She spread her thighs wide and gazed into the black space of the audience. Her chin dropped. Her eyelids closed. Her mouth went slack. Then she caught herself. That was the good thing about techno: it was a loop so she could start right where she left off. She used the pole as leverage to lift herself up to stand. The white lights could trigger a migraine, but this was no migraine. This was blindness.

She remembered Terry's megawatt smile and million-crunches abs. He snuck her into the boy's bathroom after cheerleading practice. The plan was to make out and try his dope. "'Walking on Sunshine,' Addy," he'd said.

"What?" she asked with one hand on her hip. Terry pulled her into the blue bathroom stall and removed his smooth brown belt from his plaid shorts. They dropped down past his knees. He looked slimmer than usual.

"You should've used 'Walking on Sunshine.'" He wrapped the belt around her forearm. The dope was brown and gritty, but when the fire heated it, it blackened like bubbling vinegar. Terry's arms were so veiny he didn't use the belt. He just flexed. "'Walking on Sunshine' is the best song for a cheerleading routine," he said.

He stuck the needle in her arm and it stung. The bathroom wasn't blue. It was mint-green and freezing. She shivered.

"'Walking on Sunshine' by Katrina and the Waves." The dope was a warm liquid kiss inside her skin. She nearly slipped back onto the toilet. He caught her. She laughed.

"No. We're using 'New Attitude' because it's slow enough for flips."

He turned her around to face the toilet with her back to him. He yanked on her underwear.

"Wait," she said. She snatched a condom from her makeup bag and ripped it open with her teeth. She dropped the condom. She reached down to pick it up, but there was orange piss and curly black hairs where it had landed.

The dope made her queasy. She threw up Diet Pepsi and gummy bear bile and the sweetness mixed with the piss and soap smell. She tasted dope at last: burnt vinegar and warm ash. A dark shadow moved across the bathroom. The room turned blue. She flushed the toilet and the sound was so loud, as if monsters lived in the pipes inside the walls.

Terry laughed. He didn't use spit when he put his cock in her ass. He didn't use lube. She didn't feel it or see the blood until later. Speckled lights twinkled behind her eyes. Prism zigzag light blurred the edges of the walls, of the toilet, of Terry. She saw her drool trickle from her open mouth.

"Don't."

"I don't want to get you pregnant," he said.

Her thin spit was a rainbow thread hitting the toilet water, soft and certain.

Later she'd: Bleed on toilet paper. Sit on ice. Sleep on her belly. Buy more dope from Terry. He wasn't very good at shooting her up, but Dennis could find a vein in a garbage can.

On stage at the MSC, the second song began. It was more manic and fast than the first. It was trance party music where a woman wailed about ecstasy and a little bit of you and me. Adrienne stepped out of her slinky black dress like a spider discarding its skin. Her black bra was next. She tossed it to the one man sitting up front. Her pale skin and glossed red lips and sharp cheekbones shimmered under the white lights. She stepped on her dress and tripped. She fell down onto her knees. Her black thigh-high stockings covered the tracks on the backs of her legs but they were needle sore. She slid forward and felt the hot lights pierce her neck. Her tiny swollen hands touched her small breasts. Her chest was flat as an open road; men loved that about her. She removed her black thong for the guy in the white shirt and tossed it in his direction. He removed a twenty from his pocket and set it down on the stage, where she could see it. She crawled closer to him to let him know she saw it. She removed his glasses and put them in his shirt pocket. She took his face in her fingers and wiggled it across her skin beneath her fishnet shirt. She felt his pointy nose and wet mouth brush against her nipples. She felt his slick forehead leave a greasy film on her rib cage. She loosened her bun and allowed her black hair to smack her cheeks. She watched the man's expression slide from guilt to anger, as if she'd just become his eleven-year-old niece.

"There's more where that came from," she said, tossing him her best prepubescent smile.

You should have used the song I suggested.

He said: "You should come talk to me after this song." He placed a single red carnation on the stage in front of her. She didn't look at it, but she knew it was there.

"One more song and then I'll come," she answered. Her fingers lingered on her abdomen but she wanted to scratch her arms. The itch was back.

He said: "You have the best breasts."

She stared up at the lights that opened her like a bone. She was lighter than air.

Jennifer Precious Finch

AVA STANDER is the editor of the *New York Times* best seller *Dirty Blonde*, as well as the creative director and researcher of the book *Cobain: Unseen*. Born and raised in London, England, she now lives in Los Angeles.

poppy love
by Ava Stander

I am done with heroin, but heroin is not done with me. The scars on my body may be fading, but the scars on my liver bear the evidence of my addiction. Sharing needles has infected me with hepatitis C.

The treatment I undergo for the twelve months after quitting is referred to as "chemo lite." I wake drenched in sweat with what feels like the flu times a thousand. Days and nights are spent with my head hanging over the toilet bowl, retching bile. I am a piece of hot coal lying on the cool tile floor. My skin is radioactive. My bones itch so badly it feels as though they are infested with fleas. My body's covered in wounds and scabs from scratching myself so viciously. I look like a leper. Dozens of times I think of getting loaded but I'm too stubborn to cash in the freedom I won back from the poppy.

Depression is a side effect and I catch it bad. I am unrecognizable to myself. I am reduced to a wretched, polluted amoeba unable to move from the couch. I enter suicide chat rooms online, only to be told to leave by other chatters because I am "too depressing." I plunge deeper and deeper into an abyss of desolation. All the medication and therapy in the world can't put me back together again.

It is an awful Southern Californian sunny day. The sky above me is blue, my heart is black. I have been at work for half an hour when I hear my own voice inside my head.

Drive your car off Mulholland.

I grab my purse and get into my car. Just as I escaped from the bonds of my addiction, so would I escape from this depression the past year of chemo bestowed upon me. I stop at a gas station to fill up my tank, to guarantee a fiery finish. Chain-smoking my way up the winding road of Laurel Canyon, I pass Houdini's property. I envision him immersed in a tank of water weighted down by chains, and the image won't leave my head. I drive along the serpentine twists and turns of Mulholland Drive for an hour looking for the perfect spot. I don't want to launch myself into oncoming traffic or land on anyone's house. After all, I have a conscience and don't want to hurt anyone else. I find a lookout post on a dangerous curve, with a stretch of dirt road a thousand feet long leading up to a guardrail. In it is an opening wide enough for my Honda to fit through.

I step out, into the majestic scenery of the Hollywood Hills. It is eerily quiet, as though the volume of the city had been muted. I look down and satisfy myself that the drop is sufficiently steep. I know the only way I am getting off this cliff is in a body bag.

I reverse my car to give me a good running start, but just as I reach the edge I press on the brake. I repeat this twice. My heart is punching against my rib cage. Catching my breath, fighting back tears, hands clenched around the steering wheel, I see a legal pad on the passenger seat. Should I write a goodbye note? Why bother, what I'm about to do really needs no explanation. It's a bold statement in and of itself. I'm finally going to get well. I close my eyes, put my foot on the gas, and floor it. The car takes flight, but instead of nosediving it hovers in midair for a split second, and that's when I know something has gone horribly wrong . . .

Addiction is like love. You don't know when it enters the room but you sure know when it exits. Hedonistic, idealistic, nihilistic, and above all dangerous. Have you ever been so parched that you feel like your esophagus is lined with cotton? You know that your only salvation is water, that cold, magical elixir pouring down your throat, trickling into every cell in your body. Nothing else will quench that burning need, nothing except water.

I'm not looking for God. I want to be God. I want to feel like God. Godly. My proclivity for heroin is unmatched. My affliction has been my driving force for a decade. I have traded in the glamour of Hollywood for the squalor of MacArthur Park. A neighborhood on the western edge of downtown Los Angeles, it centers around a large grassy park. Working-class Mexican and Central South American families populate the surrounding neighborhood. And then there are the undesirables. Gang members, petty criminals, ex-cons, prostitutes, pimps, the mentally sick, and the drug addicted.

I have disappeared into this milieu, only a few miles from my previous life. But the twenty-minute bus ride may as well be the distance from the earth to the moon. I left everything behind without batting an eyelash. Adapting to my surroundings. Indifferent to the consequences.

The Casa Sonora, a seedy motel a few blocks from the park that rents only to lost souls, will be the last permanent roof over my head until I get clean. My small room contains bulky, antiquated wooden furniture, carpet worn thin as cloth, and stark white walls. Cheaply framed Van Goghs that I rip out of a dime store calendar offset the funereal atmosphere.

A local gangbanger crack dealer, Spooky, sometimes stows away in my room to smoke so his homies don't find out he's getting high on his own supply. He rarely says a word. The only evidence of his presence in my room is the noise the lighter makes when he lights up. He likes that I never pester him for a hit. He is gorgeous. The ladies swoon.

On what will become my last night here, Spooky's ex-girlfriend ambushes me in the hallway. In a murderous rage, she grabs me by the throat and drags me to the banister to throw me over. I fall back into the wall and make myself as heavy as possible. When she realizes she can't lift me she unleashes punches to the back of my head, stomach, torso, and chest. I am so terrified I can't scream for help. She spits at me. I keep my head down to safeguard my face. She tries to push me down the seven flights of stairs. She tries to pry my hands open but I grip the railing with every ounce of strength I can muster and she's powerless. I don't want to die this way, murdered by someone else's hands. It is my life, mine to destroy and no one else's, and I want to live. I figure that everybody has to take a beating at some point and this is my turn. But I'll be damned if I'll let this mindless Medusa take my life. Her kicks are like a baseball bat on the side of my body. She's screaming vitriolic obscenities inches from my face. No one comes out to check on the commotion. I cling onto the railing with all the life force within me. My mouth tastes metallic. My sweat feels sticky. I look down—it's blood. Her screaming pierces my eardrums like daggers. Neither of us notice my gigantic ex-con neighbor, Cadillac, until he pulls her off me and throws her against the wall.

"You better watch yourself, bitch," she snarls, and takes off. My eyes are squeezed shut. I don't dare move. I jump at the tap on my shoulder. Cadillac asks if I need help getting back to my room. I assure him I'm okay. He treads softly back to his room as if he knows the slightest movement may cause me more pain. After an eternity, I let go of the railing. I crawl back to my room on my hands and knees, and once inside I lie down against the door and curl up in the fetal position. I fall asleep counting my bloodstained tears as they soak into the carpet. I dream of floating on waves, suspended between a starless night and the deep blue sea.

The Van Goghs frown upon me in the morning as I throw

some clothes and toiletries into my junkie luggage—a black trash bag. Miraculously, my face doesn't bear any traces of last night's homicidal attack, but the rest of me feels like I did ten rounds with Muhammad Ali. When I reach the foyer I picture myself splattered on the snow-white marble floor. My blood pouring out into the street. It sends shivers through me as though someone walked over my grave. Scoring is the first order of the day. The monster is awake and it's demanding to be fed.

I've been thrown out of every other motel in the area for nonpayment or drama. There's nowhere left to go. I'm living like a feral alley cat, in the basement of an abandoned building. I have dragged a chair and table out of the trash through the hole in the chain-link fence. The perfect setup for the day's only activities. Cooking up, shooting up, and nodding out. I can't risk being on the streets during the day. I have racked up a number of felonies and nonappearances in court, and the local cops know my face. I may as well be wearing a scarlet "A" for Addict. I'm an arrest waiting to happen. Next time I'm stopped I'm going to the pokey. And that's a hell I don't want to visit because there I would have to kick. There's no dope in jail. And that is what I fear the most.

I cop before sunrise, walking through the side streets and back alleys, passing the cardboard dwellers and sleeping bodies on the ground. After my early-morning dose of stress and anxiety, relief and gratitude pour over me once back in the safety of my living and dying room. Unwrapping the balloon takes a small forever. Who wraps these, Mexican midgets with tiny midget fingers? At long last I get the dope into the spoon. I squirt a bit of water over it and heat the mixture with my lighter to dissolve it. My needle is as dull as one of the nails used to crucify Jesus, so I sharpen it on a matchbox. The amber nectar has cooled, and I draw it into the syringe. I have to swing my arm around like a windmill to get my blood pumping. Otherwise I won't hit a vein and will end up look-ing like a bleeding pincushion.

I caress my arm in search of a vessel to carry me to oblivion. One pops up and my teeth clench as the needle goes in. I pull back the plunger and watch my blood blooming like flowers in the syringe.

The shades of my blood are ever-changing, depending on time of day, body temperature, and circumstances. I label the crimson and red hues each time they appear in the needle, like tubes of lipstick. *Scarlet Harlot, Better Red than Dead, Poppy Love, The Bride Wore Crimson, Devil's Magenta, Fuchsia Fox.* Mine are more romantic sounding than the names the makeup companies use. I push the plunger down, and before the needle's even out of my vein, my breathing slows and my heartbeat is barely there. I am God. I want to live forever. I don't want to die, I just want to stay high. My chin hits my chest. Let the drooling commence. A movie plays in my mind's eye, directed by David Lynch. In it I'm front-ing a rhythm & blues band, wearing gold lamé pedal pushers with a matching gold jacket and nothing underneath. My tiny breasts make a cameo appearance every so often. The backing vocalists are horrified. I'm singing at 33 rpm, though I should be at 45 rpm. Swaying on my gold five-inch stilettos like a wounded bull in a bullfight, bleeding out as it struggles to stay standing. The audi-ence below waits for me to keel over and die, or for the song to end, to put them and me out of our collective misery. I can't keep up but I carry on butchering the classic James Brown tune.

I feel good,
I knew that I would, now
I feel good,
I knew that I would, now
So good,

So good,
I got you.

I feel someone's presence down here with me. I lift my two-hundred-pound head up off my chest. A silhouette stands in the doorway, backlit by the unrelenting sun.

"Girl, I would knock but you ain't got a door. Girl, you in there?" The Marilyn Monroe voice belongs to Angela, a six-foot-tall Nicaraguan ladyboy. She's stunning; black cat eyes, black shiny shoulder-length hair, cherry-red lips, and legs that put any supermodel's to shame. Angela just got out from doing three months in jail. She's still in the men's clothing the county gave her upon her release. I'm annoyed she found my hideout but I try not to show it. There aren't any steps and she has to jump down onto the dirt floor.

She glances at our surroundings and asks, "How you livin'?"

"Large."

We howl with laughter and hug.

"Preciosa, give me something to wear and some whorepaint. I need to get out of this boy drag. I'm keeping a low profile until I go into this drug program in the desert. I got bumped up their waiting list cause of the SIDA. You should come with me."

SIDA is Spanish for AIDS.

"Don't be a vibe slayer," I say, raising an eyebrow and giving her my best stink eye.

"I heard about the beating you got. You should get out of the neighborhood. This place ain't no joke. Get yourself in a program. Don't you know there's nothing but hope for us until we're six feet under?"

"Hope is for suckers, Angela. And frankly, I would rather get the shit kicked out of me again than go to rehab."

Angela keeps up a steady stream of mindless chatter. I stop listening. The only way to get rid of her is to give her what she wants. I want to go back to nodding in solitude. My trash bag's hidden behind some rotting cardboard boxes. In exchange for clothes, she gives me a balloon. We prepare a shot. I fix first, before letting her use my rig. She has no problem hitting a vein. They're thick as ropes; they're all that's left of her masculinity. I'm jealous of her veins. The Marilyn voice has slowed to a purr. I light a cigarette for her and put it between her lips. Eyes closed, she smiles with every part of her face as if this were the kindest gesture anyone has ever made toward her. The first shot of dope's always the best after a period of abstinence. The cigarette falls onto the trash bag lying between her feet, and I pick it up and finish it in a few drags.

I come to some time later. It's dark and quiet. I could be the last surviving person on earth. All of Angela's happy horseshit about getting clean keeps echoing around inside my skull. I have to obliterate the thoughts. I have to do more dope to forget what I had to do to get the dope. I lead a vampiric existence—out of the sunlight during the day and into the moonlight at night. I only come out at neon. An existence as mediocre and mundane as the bourgeoisie and the nine-to-fivers I detest. My life's become so small you can barely see it under a microscope. Being a dope fiend is a twenty-four-hour-a-day job with no time off and no vacations. And the most dreadful thought of them all: *What am I doing?* That is the one thought I have to kill. I need to end this unwanted moment of clarity. I still have a tiny piece left of Angela's gift. I light a few candles and prepare another shot. Hitting a vein by the flickering light turns into a bloodbath. If the blood coagulates the heroin clogs up and won't go through the tiny opening of the spike. That's a waste I can't afford. A dozen holes later I'm in.

The girl's face staring back at me from my compact is suffering from malnutrition. My skin is diaphanous, I can almost see the bones in the front part of my skull. All I need now is lipstick and I'll look fabulous. It's not in my purse. Probably because its nestled in Angela's faux cleavage. She's an unrepentant thief.

Crouching in the wild overgrown weeds, I poke my head out of the hole in the fence to make sure the coast is clear. At dusk the air reeks of night-blooming jasmine intermingled with exhaust fumes and the infamous smog blanketing the City of Angels. Six to nine is family values time. A sea of bodies flows in and out of the local stores. A pulsating microorganism, the antithesis of the invading scary monsters and super freaks that come out after all the good people have turned in for the night. The hustle and bustle takes away my loneliness.

Waiting for the traffic light to turn green, I see a man and his young son struggling to get a cart up the steps of a building. I met Jose and Jesus selling homemade tamales outside a mini-mall where foot traffic is always heavy. When I was hungry I would stop by, and more often than not they would feed me for free. They were Christian; what Christians should be. Even though I politely decline Jose's numerous invitations to go to church, they are always happy to see me. Even though I am part of the problem, another neighborhood junkie, they don't judge and they don't ask questions.

Jose and I share a love of Pablo Neruda's poems. He told me he wooed his wife Maria by reciting them to her. These sporadic exchanges bring me close to them. Awakening a small desire in me to be "normal" again.

I hurry across the street to help, eager to do something for them for a change. When we get the cart into the lobby, Jose insists I come stay with his family for a couple of nights. My protestations fall on deaf ears. I follow them up the three flights of stairs and Jose opens the door into a small living room. The aroma of garlic and freshly cooked chicken fills the apartment. It feels like home. Maria, his wife, comes out of the kitchen and puts her arms around me.

"I'm so glad to meet you, those two have told me so much about you," she says, still holding me. She has an exquisite Roman nose, hazel eyes, and white skin. Her hair is pulled back off her face in a chignon. For a brief moment, I'm not a motherless daughter.

Grandma sits in front of the TV. She isn't thrilled. Maria leads me into the kitchen and sits me at the table. Grandma and Jose are arguing in Spanish about me staying. He comes into the kitchen and says, "Don't worry, she's just a frightened old woman who never leaves the house except on Sundays to go to church."

The walls in the small apartment are adorned with saints. It's been years since I've sat down at a table to have a meal. After dinner, Maria hands me of pair of sweats and suggests I take a shower. I do so and rejoin them. Above the television is an ornately framed picture of a saint holding two eyeballs on a plate. I ask Grandma who she is.

"Santa Lucia, the patron saint of the blind. Like you."

I am insulted by her remark, but I soon fall asleep on the couch watching TV. Much later I awake to Grandma covering me up with a blanket. I drift off again.

It's early dawn when the monster begins to stir. I come to. I panic, I have no idea where I am until I hear Grandma snoring gently. The monkey on my back is doing cartwheels on my spine. I feel my way to the bathroom, change back into my clothes, and slither away.

The streets are deserted. The neighborhood is still slumbering. I have an ominous feeling that something's amiss. As I walk down the sidewalk, I notice the same car go past me twice. It's a curb-crawler, circling me like a vulture. He pulls alongside me slowly. When the tinted window rolls down I see a man's face covered in third-degree burns.

"Are you workin'?"

I'm already too sick to turn a trick, and I yell at him to fuck off. He speeds away. My veins are ravenous. The backs of my legs are being sliced by razors. In the movie *Barbarella* there's a scene where Jane Fonda is tied to a post while a gang of mechanical dollies with sharp teeth bite at her sinewy legs. Now I'm in the leading role. With every step I take my legs grow heavier from the discomfort. I hear footsteps approaching fast. I want to run but I can't. I turn around abruptly. It's a friend from the park that goes by Willie, but I call him Abdullah after the militant character played by Bill Duke in the movie *Car Wash*. He calls me Che Guevara. He says it as one word, *Cheguevara*. Our conversations are almost always political. We are a couple of park-bench revolutionaries. Abdullah needs a gallon of vodka daily.

When I get dopesick my mood turns foul. I let loose a stream of expletives at him for scaring me. Ignoring my outburst, he fills me in on what I've missed during the two days I've spent sleeping. The police did a mass sweep of the area and arrested dozens of people. The neighborhood's hot. I tell him I have to go to the park to find Angela. She'll give me something to tide me over if she has any.

"Angela was picked up this morning," he says sadly.

We reach the park, and Abdullah is right. In the aftermath of the mass arrests nothing is jumping off. Usually at this early hour there are still a few homeless crackheads left. But it's deserted, and they have all scurried off like rats to wherever it is that rats go during daytime. The powers that be have put forth a valiant effort in the war on drugs.

The only ones here are the three wise men, sitting on their usual bench from which they run their own apothecary. They sell every kind of pill imaginable. They are the only African Americans allowed to sell in the park. But they still have to pay taxes to the local gang. The leader, Mr. James, had been a sax player when the jazz clubs were in full swing. He finally kicked his forty-year habit in exchange for a methadone maintenance program. The first time I met him he said to me, "Dope is misery."

In my youthful arrogance I shot back, "Of course it is for YOU, old man."

They make room for me on the bench. Seeing that I am in good hands, Abdullah bids his farewell and leaves for the liquor store. Midway through my tale of woe they begin discussing my financial predicament amongst themselves as if I'm not even there. Finally Mr. James turns to me.

"Because you're a hustla and you always come correct, we have decided to donate the first twenty dollars we make to your cause. This is the only time we'll ever help you out, so don't be gettin' any ideas."

There is a God after all. I thank them profusely and say to Mr. James, "You are a prince among men."

He corrects me: "No, senorita, I'm a king. Now go sit over there. I'm a superstitious fool. This is our place of business and you throw the numbers off."

I do as I am told, but not before he gives me a Klonopin to tide me over. I swallow it immediately.

I lie down in the wet grass a couple hundred yards away from them. My insides are on a slow burn; within the hour they will be boiling over into my abdomen. I can feel my blood pounding against my eardrums. I shut my eyes to stop myself from continuously checking up on the wise men. When you're jonesing, a minute lasts an hour. It's still cool, the fireball in the sky hasn't covered the neighborhood. I'm grateful for the cold chills—the sun always makes me feel worse. I can't take the suspense any longer. I open my eyes to see Mr. James walking toward me. He gives me the money, I thank him again, and I'm gone.

I score behind a dumpster in an alley, half a block from my

favorite Laundromat. It's the cleanest one I've ever been in. Whenever I enter I'm overcome by the scent of detergent. It's intoxicating. And the toilet in the bathroom is pristine, bleached as white as the heavenly clouds. I have actually eaten in there. My works are hidden in the bathroom wall in a hole at ceiling level. I no longer carry paraphernalia just in case the cops stop me. With the balloon safely tucked between my upper gum and cheek, I already feel less nauseous as I begin the walk. All I can think of is the needle going into my vein. The promise of relief, sweet euphoria, waits for me in my celestial white bathroom.

Out of the corner of my eye I see a car peel out from the curb on the other side of the street. Pulling a sharp U-turn, it comes to a stop directly in front of me. I know without looking up who it is. I have to remain calm. Staring at the ground, I continue walking. I have nothing on me anyone can find. All that stands between me and getting well is this cop obstacle. I start praying to a God I don't believe in. The car door opens, obstructing my path.

"Stop right there. Drop the purse, put your arms above your head, and face the wall."

It's Mr. Undercover. He's stopped me on many occasions and is responsible for my only arrest, which got me locked up for three days. Mr. Undercover's one of those hard-boiled film noir detectives. He picks up my purse.

"Is there anything in here I can cut myself on, any needles?"

I must stick to monosyllabic responses. If I swallow the balloon I'll have to wait for hours to shit it out. And like every junkie I have a serious case of constant constipation, a side effect of opiates. He finishes his search of my purse and hands it back to me.

"Well, Miss Hype, looks like I'm going to have to let you go."

I thank him, and the balloon falls onto my tongue. He catches a glimpse of the bright yellow color.

"What's that in your mouth?"

"Chewing gum," I answer, trying to swallow it. My throat's so dry it won't go down.

"Spit it out, NOW!"

He pulls down my bottom lip. The pain's horrific. I think he's ripped it off my face. Tears shoot out of my eyes. Stifling a scream, my mouth opens up and out plops the balloon onto the ground.

"You're under arrest."

Coming down the street are Jose, Maria, Jesus, and Grandma, dressed in their Sunday best, on their way to church. They avoid looking in my direction. I know they are averting their gaze to spare me the indignity of being handcuffed in public. Still, Jesus turns and waves at me, tugging his father's hand. Jose pulls him forward.

On the drive to the station, Mr. Undercover gets chatty. I'm not in the mood to talk. I keep wishing he would give me back my dope and drive me to my Laundromat. He won't shut up. He says drugs are just a platform for politicians to get easy votes. *Dare to Keep Kids off Drugs* is a scaremongering tactic, a lame slogan on T-shirts. Narcotics should be legal. Only pregnant users should be arrested. Addicts are only killing themselves. The CIA is responsible for flooding the ghettos with cheap cocaine to fund the Contras. This is not what he signed up for. In hindsight this all makes sense—when his division makes international headlines for corruption.

When he's done with his monologue, I ask why he won't let me go if this is such a charade.

"I got a job to do, paperwork to fill out," he replies sarcastically. We finally arrive at the dreaded cop shop. I ask Mr. Undercover if I can have one last smoke. He uncuffs me, takes a cigarette out of the packet in my purse, and lights it.

"Why are you a junkie?" he asks. I envision the scene from *The Wild One* where Johnny's asked, "What are you rebelling against?" to which he replies, "What have you got?"

With a sweeping dramatic hand gesture I declare, "Because of all this."

Without missing a beat he says, "That's just not good enough."

My Marlon Brando moment is ruined.

Sitting in the cell like a wounded animal, I recollect an argument I had with my mother in my early teens.

"It's my life to destroy," I had hissed at her.

"You can't handle freedom."

Cold turkey is taking a hold of me. The Klonopin that Mr. James gave me helps me doze off.

I'm in a holding cell inside the women's correctional facility at the Twin Towers jail in downtown Los Angeles. We call them Twisted Towers. I want to scream but I'm afraid I'll vomit. It's an infraction here in the catacombs that will get you a beatdown. There are thirty of us squashed into a sardine can made for twenty. I lie on the floor wishing that the physical pain would kill me. Wishing these feelings would kill me. I am rotting from the inside out. My guts feel like an abattoir. The symptoms of my soul sickness. The agony that stems from my heroin addiction. It's all that remains alive within me. It's all there is. I want to smash my head against the concrete floor. My skin is on fire, my every pore is being torched. My eyes are swimming in battery acid. Please, someone; please, Mr. Policeman with the gun, come in and open fire, please kill me. Put me out of my misery. For I know that even this torture I'm enduring won't stop me from going back to the poppy at the first opportunity. I'm not a victim, I'm a volunteer. I am a junkie, a bottomless pit of despair and desperation. My dreams, desires, and wishes, my hopes and ambitions all cooked up in the spoon. Lying next to me is another girl in the same shape I'm in. She reaches out to me and we hold hands.

It's five a.m. and I am on the toilet. I haven't pulled my regulation blues all the way down to my ankles, instead they rest on my thighs. I want to appear as if I'm just sitting here, because what I'm really doing is taking a shit. Even though the correctional officers are busy, they can see me. I flush immediately, so the smell doesn't linger. I wipe myself quickly. And flush again. My humiliation is palpable. It fills the tiny cell. I take a seat on the steel desk attached to the wall. A slither of bulletproof glass doubles as a window. I realize all that I have taken for granted as I gaze upon the hills.

The car plummets through trees and bushes, finally landing on a small precipice with a sonic crash. Smoke pours from the hood. I wait for the explosion that will blow me to bits, but after a couple of minutes, it fizzles out. Reality hits me. Not only am I still alive, but a fate far worse than death has befallen me. I am now carless in Los Angeles. Tears of rage lash down my face. How is it possible for one to launch oneself off a decent-size cliff and survive? The doors are jammed shut. I hurl myself out of the open window and lay sobbing on the moist ground. I want to crawl away and hide forever. It is pathetic. There is no way humanly possible of making it back up to the road. I have to call for help. I dial my friend Marie two thousand miles away in Chicago. I explain the quandary I'm in. Her words, so loving and compassionate, make me feel like an even bigger piece of shit. She is thinking logically, and calls 911. The EMTs find me almost an hour later, and strap me into a flexible stretcher, encasing my head in a contraption that prevents me from seeing anything. All I need is a ball gag and I could be the star of my own S&M movie.

The noise of the helicopter is getting closer. As it lifts me into the air, I start to spin round and round like a whirling dervish. I am pulled inside, the blinders removed, and I gaze into the face of a rather handsome medical worker. Another time, another place, I would have asked for his number. I apologize to him for wasting his time when there are others who really are sick and in need of his help. He holds my hand as I sob my way to the hospital.

Once there, I am wheeled into an emergency cubicle. The fury welling up inside me is matched in fervor only by the disappointment at having failed. A social worker informs me that I will be committed to the psychiatric unit; she asks who she can call for me. The idea of seeing those I cherish fills me with dread. She hands me a pen and paper, and reluctantly I write down some numbers. Before long, my friends start to arrive. I don't want to look at them, but my neck brace makes it impossible to turn away. The combination of painkillers and physical discomfort sends me off on a belligerent diatribe.

"I'm going to keep trying until I get it right!" I yell at them. It's cruel and spiteful. In their shoes I would've suggested a .357 Magnum for my next attempt.

My mother is the last to visit me. She is told it was an accident. I can never tell her the truth. She would be devastated to know that her only child was going to leave her all alone. She is frail and old, quietly crying over me. She was right. I can't handle freedom.

It is then, when I am faced with the anguish and sorrow I have caused to the ones I love, that I am able to take responsibility for what I have done. Responsibility is love. And I want to fall in love again. During my years in the heroin wilderness I lost my dignity, my integrity, and my self-respect. I thought that freedom meant having no ties to anyone, no possessions and no responsibility. When I was loaded there was a ten-foot wall of cotton candy between me and the world, shielding me from sadness, hopelessness, and pain. I was in my own nebula. And I didn't realize until it was too late that the sugar walls had closed in and I was trapped, a prisoner of my euphoria. Just another slave to the poppy. There is no freedom in death. I lie in the hospital bed, bound tightly by the splints and bandages, with an overwhelming rage to live.

Also available from Akashic Books

THE SPEED CHRONICLES
edited by Joseph Mattson
230, trade paperback original, $15.95

Brand-new stories by: Sherman Alexie, William T. Vollmann, James Franco, Megan Abbott, Jerry Stahl, Beth Lisick, Jess Walter, Scott Phillips, James Greer, Tao Lin, Joseph Mattson, Natalie Diaz, Kenji Jasper, and Rose Bunch.

"Akashic launches a new series of crime anthologies, each focused on a different controlled substance, with this addictive volume."
—*Publishers Weekly*

"All told, *The Speed Chronicles* deserves great praise for the audacity of the topic, the depth of the discussion, the diversity of its voices, and plain, old, good storytelling." —*New York Journal of Books*

THE COCAINE CHRONICLES
edited by Gary Phillips & Jervey Tervalon
288 pages, trade paperback, $15.95

Brand-new stories by: Susan Straight, Lee Child, Ken Bruen, Laura Lippman, Nina Revoyr, Jerry Stahl, Bill Moody, Emory Holmes II, James Brown, Gary Phillips, Jervey Tervalon, Kerry E. West, Donnell Alexander, Deborah Vankin, Robert Ward, Manuel Ramos, and Detrice Jones.

"The best stories in *The Cocaine Chronicles* . . . are equal to the best fiction being written today."
—*New York Journal of Books*

"The perfect stocking stuffer for your uncle in AA."
—*New York Observer*

LOS ANGELES NOIR
edited by Denise Hamilton
320 pages, trade paperback original, $15.95

Brand-new stories by: Michael Connelly, Janet Fitch, Susan Straight, Hector Tobar, Patt Morrison, Emory Holmes II, Robert Ferrigno, Gary Phillips, Christopher Rice, Naomi Hirahara, Jim Pascoe, Scott Phillips, Diana Wagman, Lienna Silver, Brian Ascalon Roley, and Denise Hamilton.

• A *Los Angeles Times* best seller, Book Sense Notable Pick, and SCIBA Book Award winner!

• Featuring the 2008 Edgar Award–winning story "The Golden Gopher," by Susan Straight.

BROOKLYN NOIR
edited by Tim McLoughlin
366 pages, trade paperback original, $15.95

Brand-new stories by: Pete Hamill, Sidney Offit, Arthur Nersesian, Pearl Abraham, Ellen Miller, Maggie Estep, Adam Mansbach, CJ Sullivan, Chris Niles, Norman Kelley, Nicole Blackman, and others.

"*Brooklyn Noir* is such a stunningly perfect combination that you can't believe you haven't read an anthology like this before. The writing is flat-out superb, filled with lines that will sing in your head for a long time to come."
—Laura Lippman, winner of the Edgar, Shamus and Agatha awards

BOSTON NOIR
edited by Dennis Lehane
256 pages, trade paperback original, $15.95

Brand-new stories by: Dennis Lehane, Stewart O'Nan, Patricia Powell, John Dufresne, Lynne Heitman, Don Lee, Russ Aborn, J. Itabari Njeri, Jim Fusilli, Brendan DuBois, and Dana Cameron.

• Featuring Dana Cameron's Anthony Award and Macavity Award–nominated story "Femme Sole," Brendan Dubois's Shamus Award–nominated story "The Dark Island," and Dennis Lehane's Anthony Award–nominated story, "Animal Rescue."

SAN FRANCISCO NOIR
edited by Peter Maravelis
232 pages, trade paperback original, $15.95

Brand-new stories by: Barry Gifford, Robert Mailer Anderson, Michelle Tea, Peter Plate, Kate Braverman, Domenic Stansberry, David Corbett, Eddie Muller, Alejandro Murguia, Sin Sorracco, Alvin Lu, John Longhi, Will Christopher Baer, Jim Nisbet, and David Henry Sterry.

San Francisco Noir lashes out with hard-biting tales exploring the shadowy nether regions of scenic "Baghdad by the Bay." In this superb collection, virtuosos of the genre meet up with the best of SF's literary fiction community to chart a unique psycho-geography for a dark landscape.